GayLords Inn

FOR LITERARY HEAT

www.barbarianspy.com

WARNING: This book is for sale to **ADULT AUDIENCES ONLY**. Contains graphic gay male sex, multiple partners, anal sex, nongraphic violence, and gay love and romance, all of which may be considered offensive by some readers.

All sexually active characters in this work are at least 18 years of age.

BarbarainSpy
Toronto, Australia

GayLords

Inn

habu

Table of Contents

(Note: The named gay male Kama Sutra positions in this
book are keyed to those in the Web site
http://gaysexpositionsguide.com/)

Characters, Alphabetically by First Name

(Chapters found in)

Adam Vance—Inn guest, New York model (5, 6)

Alex Renard—Co-owner of GayLords Inn, New Yorker, French Canadian stock, chef (all chapters)

Allen Gerhardt—Inn guest, TV comedian (2, 3)

Andy Wilson—Inn guest, Trenton, New Jersey, high school soccer player (2)

Averett Gerhardt—Allen Gerhardt's brother from Indiana (3)

Brad Taggert—GayLords Inn reception clerk (3, 4, 5, 6)

Chris Clarke—rentboy (4, 5, 6)

Claude Overby—Cape May doctor (3, 6)

Colin—Inn guest, boy toy and employee of Frank Hosler (5, 6)

Cory Townsend—Inn guest, Baltimore TV anchorman (2, 3, 4)

David Pollack—Cape May police detective-lieutenant (2, 3, 4, 6)

Deep Diver—Inn guest, male porn actor (3)

Dieter Baum—Inn guest, New York jeweler (5, 6)

Denny Walker—Inn guest, porn film cameraman (3)

Derek Hillsman—Martin Beardsley's media consultant (2, 3, 4)

Eddie Renard—Brother to Alex, Cape May cruise boat captain (1, 3, 5, 6)

Edwin MacAlister—Cape May deputy mayor (5)

Felippe Martinez—Inn guest, defense contractor company CEO, father of Scott Martinez (5, 6)

Frank Hosler—Inn guest, grocery chain CEO, accompanied by Kurt and Colin (5, 6)

Hakim Maroff—GayLords Inn room and dining room attendant and masseur (5)

Hal Burton—Inn guest, porn film director (3, 4)

Hanyu Li—Inn guest, porn movie company's Mr. Fixit (3, 4)

Jack Doff—Inn guest, male porn actor (3)

Jack Wilder—Inn guest, Philadelphia lawyer (2, 3)

Jeff Stockdon—GayLords Inn reception clerk and masseur (2, 3)

Joshua Sinclair—Inn guest, New York theater producer (5, 6)

Jock Johnson—Inn guest, Martin Beardsley's campaign manager (2, 3)

Kent Dolan—Car thief on the run from Texas (3)

Kurt—Inn guest, boy toy and employee of Frank Hosler (5, 6)

Martin Beardsley, Inn guest, U.S. senatorial candidate serving in the Maryland legislature (2, 3)

Mel Duncan—Inn guest, cross dresser, Philadelphia lawyer (2, 3, 4, 5, 6)

Neal Ehlers—New York fashion photographer (5, 6)

Peter Randal—Trenton, New Jersey, police detective (3)

Raif DuCorde—Black Jamaican, GayLords Inn handyman (2, 3, 4, 5, 6)

Ricky Sanchez—Hispanic, GayLords Inn room and dining room attendant (2, 3, 4, 5, 6)

Sam Sterling/Snake—Inn guest, rock star (2, 3, 4)

9

Scott Martinez—Inn guest, with Tye Grant (5, 6)

Sean Temple—Co-owner of GayLords Inn, Californian, former collegiate gymnast (all chapters)

Stan Brown—New York gym owner (4)

Ted Landon—Inn guest, pro tennis player (2, 3, 4)

Tex—Inn guest, Fort Worth, Texas, bounty hunter (3)

Tom Miller—Inn guest, Trenton, New Jersey, high school soccer coach (2, 3)

Tony Taylor—Inn guest, New York stage actor (5)

Tye Grant—Inn guest, with Scott Martinez (5, 6)

Val Thomas—Transvestite, GayLords Inn room and dining room attendant (2, 3, 4)

Chapter One: Closing the Deals

"Sorry, is this seat taken? The place seems to be filled up this morning."

"Certainly, no problem. Have a seat. I was about finished anyway." Alex looked at the younger man sitting down across from him at the outdoor area of Avalon Coffee on Gurney, just in from Beach Street in Cape May. The guy asking if he could share the table didn't look like New Jersey, even in the summer. His hair was frosted and he looked like a California surfer, a wild-colored sports shirt above short, tight, white shorts and leather sandals. All sun in appearance. That said he looked real good.

"Great weather, isn't it?"

"Yeah, but a lot more humid than where I'm from," Sean answered. He'd looked over the opportunities before he'd requested to sit with any of the singles at the table. The tall—got to be six and a half feet—burly hunk with the flaming red hair, even though it was lightening up at the temples—mid to late thirties maybe?—had been the best possibility by far.

"Oh, where's that?" Alex asked.

"California. L.A."

Bingo, Alex thought. "Well, it's a lot nicer here than where I've just come from."

"Where's that?" Sean asked, blowing on his coffee, obviously pleased that the other guy had put his hand up requesting another cup of joe.

"Hyde Park, New York. You know, where the Roosevelts' place is. Not where I'm really from, though. I'm French Canadian. Long line of fur trappers."

That would be one of my guesses, Sean thought. Big and rough looking—but in a good way; a great way. And evidence of fur at the neckline of the T-shirt that fit his sculpted chest close.

"Just graduated from the CIA there and—"

"The CIA? The spooks train there?" Sean asked in disbelief. "And you can talk about it?"

Alex laughed. "The Culinary Institute of America."

"Chefs? You're a chef? A big, strapping guy like you?"

Alex looked harder, and with greater interest at the surfer type sitting across from him. Was he sending out signals? "Yeah, I'm a chef now. I'm in Cape May looking for a business to start."

"I'm here looking for a business to start too," Sean said. "My name's Sean, by the way."

"I'm Alex. What do you do?"

Anything you want me to do, big, hairy guy, was what Sean thought, but his answer was, "Well, I haven't done anything for a while. I was a kept man."

Alex gave him a quizzical look. That has got to be a statement of preference.

"Heard of the TV actor and racecar driver, Tommie Wells? He was my partner. Ran into a tree a year ago. Left me a bundle, but with a need to find something to do." There, I've laid it down, Sean thought. If I'm right and this guy is gay, this might be my lucky night.

"Sure, I've heard of Wells," Alex answered. "Sorry to hear it. So, will you . . . I mean what do you do?" There's a signal, if I've ever heard one, Alex thought.

12

Wells was a power top. So, is this cute Sean guy telling me that he is—?

"Can't very well do what I did at Southern Cal," Sean said. "I was a gymnast. Almost made the Olympics one year. There's no career in that, though, unless you go into coaching. And you really need to have earned some medals to do that. My interests now are quite different. In L.A. I dabbled in antiques—not the usual California antiques, which are anything over five years old—but early Americana. It's part of why I came east. Was tired of all of the Tommie Wells stuff, though, and people then automatically knowing I am gay, which is another reason."

What Alex took from that was the gymnast and gay parts. Athletic, flexible. Interesting. Sweet. And forward. He seemed to be on the make. "I know how that is," Alex ventured. Time for a signal of my own. Wonder if he can take it blunt. "That's why I'm here looking to pick up a business of my own. I'm tired of working for bosses and companies that want to tell me who I can nail or not— what guy I can screw or not."

Sean, who had been looking out on the street, snapped his head back. Goddamn, he's telling me he's gay—a power top. He's hitting on me—well, back at me. Sean couldn't suppress a grin.

"So, maybe you don't really want to sit at my table?" Alex added. ". . . unless you're shopping in my store."

"Your table is just fine," Sean answered, giving Alex a level look.

"My bed is even better," Alex said.

"I'm into furniture, so tables and beds are all good," Sean answered, with a smile.

"Looks like we're being given the evil eye by the waiters," Alex said, looking around the café, giving Sean a moment to absorb what they both knew Alex was laying down. "People are standing around looking for seats."

"But the coffee you ordered hasn't arrived yet."

"That's OK. I was going to leave before that anyway."

"Yes, you were. And I disrupted that."

"You didn't disrupt anything," Alex said, giving Sean a hard look. Sean blushed and looked down. When he raised his head, he was smiling.

"I'm taking a stroll up Ocean Street, taking in some of the antique stores," Sean said. "I know it isn't your thing, but would you like—?"

"Sure, I had no plans this afternoon. I can use the exercise of a walk. And antique stores would save any taxing of my wallet."

Later, at dusk, they were walking the surf line along the Cape May beach, sandals and boots in hand and chattering away on topics neither one could remember later other than that the details had become progressively more personal and intimate.

"It got dark awfully fast," Sean said at last. "It's almost supper time. Would you like to catch something with me?"

I'd like to do something to you, Alex thought, but what he said was, "Sure, a guy has to eat to keep his strength up . . . to be able to do vigorous activity . . . and all."

"Like antique hunting?" Sean said.

"You don't look like an antique to me," Alex responded.

They both laughed. But they both knew what was being suggested, what was being negotiated. They stopped, fingers of surf rolling around their feet. Sean pulled in closer to Alex' side, and Alex put an arm around Sean's waist. Sean turned his face up, Alex his face down, and they kissed.

"Look, this is some sort of decision point, I think," Alex said. "I'm a power top and I'm demanding—

unusually demanding. If this isn't going to go the distance, we probably should—"

"What restaurant?" Sean asked.

"There's the Martini Beach at the corner of Beach and Decatur," Alex answered, with a grin. "But, better, there's my brother's place on Benton. That's where I'm staying while I'm trying to buy a business here. He's taken a charter cruise down the coast. He'll be gone for three days. I'll fix us a meal you'll never forget. I'm a chef, remember?"

"And then?"

"And then, if you don't want to walk away right now, I'll fuck you for three days in ways you'll never forget. It's got to be what you want. It sure as hell is what I want. Haven't we been waltzing around this negotiation enough? Isn't it time for beddy bye?"

Sean shuddered, but he raised his face again to receive the kiss that sealed the deal.

As they kissed, Alex ran a hand under the waistband of Sean's shorts in back, gliding his hand down and running his finger into the crease. Sean came up on his toes in acceptance, and the kiss became more intense. Alex rubbed his index finger along Sean's hole a couple of times and then entered it.

Groaning, Sean whispered. "Fuck me. Fuck me here, if you want."

Alex laughed a low, guttural laugh. He started to move his finger in and out, and Sean shuddered and held on tight to him.

* * * *

"Fuck! Shit! Yes! Nail me hard! Work me. Nail my ass, you big stud! God, it's huge! I've never been fucked in a position this athletic before. Work me hard."

Alex was sitting on the bed, legs stretched out in front of him, Sean cantilevered over Alex' legs, facing away from Alex like the figurehead on a sailing ship, his legs streaming around Alex' hips and back, with Alex grasping Sean's wrists, pulling the younger man's arms back hard, and arching Sean's back toward him. Alex' cock was buried in Sean's passage, and Alex was pumping him with deep stabs of his hips.

They'd stumbled into the bedroom, fumbling at each other's clothes, and didn't initially make it to the bed. Alex first fucked Sean up against the wall, his hands gripping and spreading Sean's butt cheeks to aid in Sean being able to sheath the thickness of Alex' erection. Sean's knees were hooked on Alex' hips and one of his hands was buried in the red hair of Alex' head and the other in the thick matting on Alex' chest, and the two were deep kissing as Alex humped the younger man against the wall to an ejaculation by both.

Standing there, in place, both panting hard, Sean murmured, "That was good."

"It *is* good," Alex answered. "And it's gonna be great. You claim to have been a gymnast. I'm gonna put you through your paces. Have you ever been through the positions of the gay Kama Sutra? I like to fuck the positions of the Kama Sutra."

And he did. After the flying fuck position on the bed, they did the Crab—more than one position of it. First, Alex was on his back, with Sean on top of him, facing him and on his cock. Sean was cantilevered back toward Alex' feet, in a crouch position, one hand jacking his cock and the other one with a fist buried in the mattress behind him to hold him in position. Alex was grabbing Sean's thighs to keep him steady there. Half way through that fuck position, Alex turned Sean on the cock, so that Sean was full on top of Alex, both running the same way, but hovering over him, his legs bent and feet flat on the mattress and his arms stiff and holding up his torso. Alex gripped his waist with both hands and slammed Sean up and down on his cock. Before the mutual shoot off, the Crab position collapsed into what Alex muttered was called the Pearly Gates, Sean collapsed on top of Alex, an arm wrapped up and around Alex' head, the faces of the two turned to each other in a deep kiss, Sean's legs bent back for leverage as he fucked himself on Alex' cock and Alex jacked his cock.

"Great position," Sean murmured.

"My favorite finisher, but we're nowhere close to finishing," Alex answered. Sean shuddered at the prospect.

After a brief respite, Alex took Sean in an Afternoon Delight at the dresser. Sean, facing Alex, was stiffed armed down onto the front edge of the dresser to hold his body suspended. His legs were fully bent, with Alex standing between them, Sean's ankles on Alex' shoulders, and Alex cupping the back of Sean's neck with one hand and Sean's chin with the other, to come in periodically for a kiss, while Alex pounded Sean's ass. After Sean released his load, Alex gathered up Sean and, continuing to pump inside the younger man's ass, frog-marched him across to the bed, lowered him in a full stretch on the bed, lifted one of Sean's legs for deeper access, and continued fucking him in a side split version of the Leg Glider.

"God, you are flexible, aren't you? That was great," Alex declared.

"I've never had such hot sex—and such a big dick," Sean answered in a nearly exhausted voice.

Spent for the moment, the two lay in a stretched-out embrace, each still working the other's cock, both slowly regaining a regular breathing pattern.

"Whew, that was an athletic workout and a great fuck," Sean said again, awe clear in his voice on what Alex could do with his body—the flexibility he could challenge.

"Nope," Alex murmured.

"Nope?"

"It wasn't 'was' a great fuck—it's an ongoing part of a great fuck. Ever done Bumper Cars?"

"Bumper what? Oh, what? Shit! Oh, fuck, oh, fuck!"

Alex turned Sean on his belly and stretched out on top of him, in reverse. cradling Sean's head between his feet, grabbing Sean's ankles with his fists, thrusting down into Sean's channel in the reverse of the normal penetration, and beginning to pump again. Alex turned this into a Soaring Eagle, jack-knifing Sean's legs up into his chest, and Alex in a push-up position on top of him in reverse penetration, using his arms stiff extended into the mattress for leverage in the rise and fall of the cock inside Sean.

"Enough, enough!" Sean cried out as Alex was dragging him over to the side of the bed for yet another testing position.

Alex let loose of him and let him roll over onto his side on the bed. Alex sat, cross-legged on the bed, looking down at the panting younger man.

"God, that is one big cock," Sean murmured.

"Helps with some of the more exotic positions," Alex said. "You're doing great."

"Doing great?" Sean exclaimed. "Do you mean—?"

Alex reached a hand toward him, and Sean moaned a deep moan. "Ever done the Flying Spider?"

"Please no, no more for now. You're killing me. Besides, you invited me here for dinner. You said you'd fix me a great meal."

"So, you want to take a break to eat? Sure, we can do that. I'll fix you something that will energize you. After eating dinner, I'll show you what eating ass is. Then we'll fuck again."

Sean groaned and turned onto his back, flinging his arm over his face. "Yes, after dinner we'll fuck again. Call me when dinner is ready. I'll just lie here until then and groan."

* * * *

"You'll be bidding against me?" Alex exclaimed when he saw Sean walk up to the large gingerbread Victorian house on Decatur that Alex was about to enter.

"You're bidding on this property too?" Sean asked. "I thought you wanted to open a restaurant. This is much too big for that."

"And I thought you wanted to open an antique store."

"I was really thinking of a B&B that sold antiques on the public floor," Sean answered.

"I was thinking of a B&B too," Alex said. "One B is for breakfast. I hadn't decided whether to add lunch or dinner."

"So, we're looking for the same thing."

"I think we both got what we were looking for last night," Alex said.

"Far beyond my fondest dream," Sean answered. "I didn't think I was going to be able to walk here today."

"Complaining?"

"Not on your life. You took me to heaven and then to hell and back to heaven. I have *never* been fucked like that before."

"I heard that Tommy Wells was real good at cocking. I figured you could take it. I know you told me about him because everyone knows he was a power top."

19

"Not as good as you. But what are we going to do about this property? If we're bidding against each other, it will just run the price up needlessly to where neither of us can afford it."

"I can't afford it anyway," Alex said. "It's just a dream for me. I don't have the capital."

"I've got a bundle burning a hole in my bank account," Sean said.

"So, there's that then," Alex said. "You get it by default."

"Not so fast," Sean said. "You're a chef. I'd need one. As you said, one of the Bs in B&B is for 'breakfast.' I can do the bed part, the front of house. You would need that. You can take care of the food. We could go into it together."

"Yeah, maybe we could."

"I want it to be a gay-friendly place," Sean said.

"I want it to be a gay-exclusive place," Alex countered. "A gay-insistent place. I want guys to feel free to fuck in their rooms and make noise at it, if they want. I want gay guys to have someplace here they'll feel totally comfortable in. I don't want them coming to the place unless they intend to come in the rooms."

"Like the noise you pulled out of me last night?"

"Fucked you good, didn't I?" Alex grinned.

"Fucked me great." Sean grinned back. "So, that would be fine with me, as long as it didn't keep antique browsers out of the public areas during normal store hours. And it fits in with the name I was thinking of. How about GayLords Inn? Catching, I thought, and a clear welcome to those we'd be targeting."

"It's good to go for me. Shall we go in and buy this sucker together?"

"I'm game."

"And then we'll go back to my brother's house and I'll fuck your lights out. Ever done a Pile Driver."

20

Sean groaned. "As a matter of fact, I have."

"Will you let me? . . . I think you've figured out what I like to do."

"Yes, I'm finding you quite invigorating and fulfilling, but I think there's one thing I need to establish with you, especially as it looks like we're going to be business partners too."

"And what is that?"

"I enjoy you fucking me in all those inventive positions, but I wasn't built to be monogamous. I could promise you I would be, but I couldn't keep to it. I never have been able to."

"I'm relieved to hear you say that, actually. I'm the same way. I just thought I'd try not being that way. But this will be great."

"This?"

"Fucking you in an open relationship. It will make swinging you all the more arousing."

"Swinging me?"

"I'll keep it a secret from you until we get to my brother's house." Alex was grinning. Sean found that contagious and couldn't help grinning back.

* * * *

Sean was panting hard, decelerating from having been introduced to the basement room in Alex' brother's house on Benton Street. There had been an actual swing. Alex had sat in it, naked, and drawn Sean, also naked, onto his lap, facing him, with Alex' cock buried in Sean's passage. They had both grabbed hold of the chains attaching the swing seat to the high ceiling, and Sean had learned that either one of them had to provide pelvis power as Alex sent them swinging in the air in what Alex called an extreme Lap Dance. The swinging motion itself was fucking Sean on the cock.

21

Later, Sean experienced another form of the swinging fuck, as Alex put him in a black leather sling, bound his wrists and ankles on the chains holding the sling to the ceiling, and gave him his cock, hard and deep.

A "Hello, I'm home early," sounded through the house and Sean—but not Alex tensed in surprise.

"It's just Eddie, back from the sea. If you like my cock, you'll love his. And excited by something even hairier than I am?"

Before Sean could answer, the charter boat captain was standing in—and filling up—the doorway to the room. He was sporting a big grin and a pair of shorts, and nothing else. He was, indeed, hairier than Alex was, but just as tall, muscular, and burly. He was bearded, the red of his hair and the mop on his head and the matting of chest—and Sean soon found out, his pubic hair—flamed as bright as that of his brother.

Sean's first thought was to be shocked that Alex' brother found Alex and him in this compromising position, but then it hit him that the sex equipment filling this room was the brother's, not Alex'. He moaned in anticipation of what could happen here. Looking at the big hunk as Eddie stood in the door and took Sean's naked body under assessment, Sean was melting in expectation. Did he want Alex' brother inside him? What if the brothers wanted to do him together?

Already the man had unzipped, flared his shorts and pulled out his cock.

Yes, Sean wanted him.

"Good news, Eddie," Alex said. "Sean here and I are business partners. Just bought a big mansion on Decatur to put a B&B in. And better news—neither one of us wants to be monogamous. You want to fuck him, big brother?"

"Well, sure I want to fuck him . . . if he's willing."

Alex turned and looked at Sean. "Is this what you mean by an open relationship?"

"Yes, I want him to fuck me," Sean answered.

"Not here," Alex said, as he started releasing Sean's wrists and ankles. "Eddie and I aren't into that sharing shit. I fucked you here tonight, so he won't fuck you here tonight."

"Ah, come on, bro. I do some of my best work in this room."

"Not my business partner. Not tonight; not your usual shit," Alex answered in a firm voice.

"OK, if you insist," Eddie answered, with a laugh.

Alex stood aside as Eddie came over, scooped Sean up without so much as a grunt, tossed him over his shoulder, and went up to the master bedroom. He tossed Sean on the bed, slapped his thighs opened, and lowered his body between the smaller man's legs. Sean arched his back and opened his mouth in one long, deep moan as Eddie, seemingly even thicker than Alex, entered and entered and entered him.

The strong man of the sea fucked forever. When he was finished—not using any of the Kama Sutra techniques of Alex but relying on straightforward positions giving him the best angle and depth, he was stretched on top of Sean, pinning the smaller, lighter man to the bed. He had an arm under Sean's neck and cupped his chin with the other hand, tilted it up, and gave Sean a passionate kiss.

"That was nice. Are you going to visit me here when you have time from correcting all my brother's mistakes in running that B&B?"

"If you come home from sea occasionally and visit me at the B&B."

"Deal. And, Sean . . ."

"Yes?"

"Here it comes again."

23

"Oh, shit, yes. Yes, yes, yes." Mooooann.

When Sean managed to get out of the bed while Eddie was showering, he pulled on the robe Eddie had slung over a chair; looked in the bedroom where Alex had been sleeping; and, not seeing him there, padded downstairs—all the way to the basement. Alex had a young guy—here apparently by magic this late at night, trussed up in the sling, and was merrily fucking away. Sean only later learned that Eddie had brought the guy back to the house for himself, and he'd been in the kitchen, eating a sandwich when Eddie took Sean upstairs.

So, Sean thought, we need no more proof than this—from both Alex and me—that we're both good with a wide-open relationship.

When he returned to the bedroom, Eddie grabbed him by the wrist as he entered the room, slapped him up against the wall, grabbed him where his thighs met his buttocks, and lifted and set him down on a raging erection. As Eddie fucked him hard against the wall, Sean let loose of all of his inhibitions and fucked the hairy giant back.

Chapter Two: Opening Day

The Kitchen (First floor, left rear)

"For Christ sake, what is your problem, Val?" Alex slammed the knife he was using to slice the pound cake for Sunday's breakfast down on the counter in the kitchen of the B&B and grabbed the Goth transvestite, who was supposed to be polishing up the silverware, by the studded belt at her back and shook her.

"It's just all too chaotic," Val sobbed. "There's just too much that needs to be done."

Alex let loose of her, setting her down in front of the silverware she was supposed to be polishing. She sauntered off to rearrange the coffee urn and the toaster.

"Which won't be done the way you are flouncing around. Just settle down, take a breath, and get back to work."

"Well, shit," Val exclaimed. "Now I've broken a nail. I knew I should have called in sick today. And Ricky, he yelled at me while we were finishing making the beds upstairs. And I can't sleep in the same room he's in. He snores and it isn't right for a lady to be sleeping—"

"OK, that's enough, Val. I know what you need. I knew I'd have to do it for the kitchen to run properly anyway. I don't have time today, but a quickie should settle you down." He grabbed Val again and hustled her into the pantry. Struggling with her, he managed to pull her panties down and off her legs.

"What are you doing? Oh, no! Not that."

"What you need is a good put-in-your-place fucking," Alex declared. "You knew when you took this job that you'd be sleeping with the guests occasionally—and me, as I wanted it."

"I know, I know. But I didn't think. Oh, God, what are you doing?"

"Lean into the shelf. I like to use Kama Sutra positions. This, in case you're interested, is the Danseur. Once I've mastered you, this is going to be a much-better working kitchen. Might as well do it from the get go."

He had Val on one leg and leaning into a pantry shelf. He had his left arm laced under Val's armpit and right leg, which extended up Val's chest like she was doing a high kick. Alex' left hand was flipping the top of a Crisco can open, prepared to use what was at hand to lube the transvestite's ass up.

"No, please, wait. I've never—"

"You've never what?"

"I've never been fucked." It came out in a sob. "I wanted this job. And I want to be fucked. It just hasn't happened yet. If you fuck me, go slow, please."

"Oh, for Christ sake. I can't fuck you for your first time like this." Disgusted, Alex dropped Val's leg, stooped down, swept up her panties, and handed them back to her. "You can't work in this B&B unless you're willing to play. Sean and I made that quite clear when we hired you."

"I know, I know," Val murmured through snuffles. "And I want it. I really do. It just hasn't happened yet."

"Ten o'clock tonight, my room in the Christopher Isherwood Suite. We'll go through it all. I'll break you in as gently as I can. But you knew what kind of B&B this was before you took the job. If you change your mind, don't show up there or for work in the morning."

Val sniffed. "Yes, Mr. Renard. I'll be there. I want to work here. And I want what you and Mr. Temple are trying to provide here."

"Good. We need you here in the morning. Our first day open and we have a full house. Now, buck up and get to the silverware. I'm going out to see if the painting is done."

Front Walk of the GayLords Inn

"Ah, I was just about to come get you, Alex. Raif has finished with the touch-up painting. Doesn't it look great? Enough of a statement?"

Alex joined his business partner and frequent bed partner, Sean Temple, out on the walk and turned to look back at the front of the B&B. He laughed. GayLords Inn was a twenty-eight-room Victorian mansion on Cape May's Decatur Street not more than four blocks from the Atlantic Ocean. By custom, all of the Victorian mansions in the historic part of town were painted in bright, attention-getting colors. GayLords would out-glare them all now, at least until the paint weathered. The house was painted in baby blue, trimmed in bright pink. The handyman, a black bull muscle-bound Jamaican with dreadlocks, Raif DuCorde, had just finished touching up the trim work.

Raif had been hired as much for what would be his obvious appeal to some of the guests—and because Sean had sampled him and found him quite satisfactory—as for his handiwork skills. But a twenty-eight room mansion with a swimming pool in the side terrace was going to keep him busy. Room and board came with the job and he had been assigned, appropriately, Sean thought, to the Diesel Washington Room on the attic floor, left, front.

Once the B&B got going good, though, Sean didn't expect Raif to be spending many of his nights in his own bedroom. Truth be known, Sean expected Raif to be spending an occasional night in his bedroom, one of three rooms in the Christopher Isherwood Suite across the rear of the second floor, in which he and Alex each had a bedroom and bath and shared a linking sitting room.

Raif was crouched half way up the side stairs of the front porch and was talking with one of the guests who had already arrived and was sitting in a rocker on the porch, strumming a guitar. The guest had signed in and provided a credit card in the name of Sam Sterling. But when he arrived both Sean and the reception clerk, Jeff Stockdon, had recognized him as the lead singer who went by the name of Snake for a popular rock band. Sean was amused that he had reserved the Freddy Mercury Suite on the second floor, front, right, which included a tower room.

He wasn't the only guest who had arrived. Cory Townsend, who Sean had recognized as a thirty-year-old TV anchorman in Baltimore, had arrived as clandestinely as he could and gone straight to the Don Lemon Room, a smaller one on the third floor, left, middle. His room had a shower rather than a full bath. He had been holed up there since he'd arrived. There had been rumors he was gay, but obviously he didn't want to feed them, in which case, Jeff said, he probably shouldn't have come to a B&B that was advertising in gay magazines as a "no-holds-barred" gay activity friendly place to stay in the historical beach resort town of Cape May.

Two others, to Jeff Stockdon's amusement, had also arrived and were holed up in the attic. One, Mel Duncan, arriving in full hunting gear even though all of the wild areas around Cape May were designated wildlife habitats, had requested the Renée Richard's Suite at the rear of the attic. Arriving a half hour later, prominently

28

displaying a pair of binoculars and declaring loudly that he was here to do some bird watching, was Jack Wilder, who had requested the Rock Hudson Suite at the right, front of the attic. The two didn't fool anyone at GayLords, though, and Alex hoped that guests would be comfortable enough in the future not to try ruses like this. Both men were middle aged, they had booked suites with a connecting door on the same day, and their reservation e-mails had letterheads from the same law office in Philadelphia.

Unbeknownst to the owners and staff of GayLords—none of whom would care a bit anyway—Mel wasn't now off hunting and Jack wasn't busy spying on birds. At this moment, Mel, in full women's battle gear, including a wig, makeup, a garter belt, black stockings, and spike heels, was lying on the bed in the Rock Hudson Suite, a bed the two found they had to pull away from the wall to avoid the attention of everyone else in the building wondering what the knocking sound was. His stockinged legs were raised and spread, and his dress was bunched up around his waist as his law partner, Jack Wilder, lay between his legs and missionary fucked him.

The pro tennis player, Ted Landon, was already tucked away in the Cole Porter Suite, third floor front, right, including a tower room, and was agonizing over a music composing pad. He was aging out of the tennis circuit, he had admitted to Alex in a stammering voice, and wanted to try his hand at music composition. Alex had complimented him on his tennis playing, his looks, his physique, and as he had him up against the wall of his suite, his sexiness. Landon had enjoyed the attention, and thus the first guest fucked in the B&B on opening day was by Alex testing out the flexibility of the athlete by giving him the position he called the Elevated Spits. Landon did the splits on the dresser in his room, facing the mirror and holding himself steady with his fists pressed to the dresser top in front of him, while big Alex—big in several dimensions—held his hips and fucked him from behind.

Although Landon had claimed he would be composing in private this afternoon, the likelihood was that he was stretched out on his back on the bed in the Cole Porter Suite, moaning the Kama Sutra position Alex had put him into. All was fine, though. Landon admitted he's come to the B&B in the hope of some attention that wouldn't make him so "my tennis career is over," and Alex had left assuring him that as long as he had the flexibility to do the splits on top of a dresser and to take a cock deep he still was in great shape.

In a flurry of other activity just a few minutes before, Martin Beardsley, a U.S. senatorial candidate serving in the Maryland legislature, had trundled in with his middle-aged black campaign manager, Jock Johnson, and his much younger media consultant, Derek Hillsman. Hillsman was young enough that Stockdon checked his driver's license. Beardsley had reserved two rooms of the premier Alexander the Great Suite, third floor, rear for himself and the second, attached bedroom and bath of that suite for his media consultant, Hillsman. Johnson was booked into the Brian Boitano Suite on the same floor, front, left.

When they entered the B&B, Beardsley was protesting loudly that he had no idea what sort of inn Johnson had booked them into—but he accepted the suite key without fuss, put an arm around young Hillsman's shoulders, and mounted the stairs.

Alex, Sean, and Jeff all stood in the foyer, smiling and watching the three men going up the stairs, knowing for certain that there would be more than stairs mounted in the near future. Jeff, a thirty-something laid-back hippy type with a surfer's muscular body and beach bum blond hair, put his tongue in the side of us mouth and produced a loud popping sound.

Alex spoke up. "Yeah, the guy is young, but I doubt he's a virgin and his male cherry is being popped this afternoon. He was swinging his little butt like he wanted what he's going to get and has gotten it before." The tone of his voice was almost one of admiration. He was already scheming how he was going to get a piece of that before the weekend was over. Truth be known, so was Jeff Stockdon.

The last but two of the guests who filled up the B&B on its first, Saturday, night in business was sitting on the front porch, at some distance from where the rock star and Raif were in deep conversation. He was looking morose and entirely unhappy to be here or anywhere else at the moment. Allen Gerhardt, the TV comedian, had been assigned to the Elton John Suite, second floor, front, left. He had started to check in incognito, but Sean, not knowing he'd used a credit card in another name, and recognizing him from TV, had welcomed him with his true name. Gerhardt had looked devastated since then, but he'd stayed.

After the man had gone to his room and then down to the front porch to sit, slowly rock, and implode into himself, Sean had also felt miserable. He had committed a mistake by not checking on who the guest wanted to be while at the B&B. It was a basic service—privacy to be and do as the man wished—that GayLords intended to provide. And worse than that, he remembered why Gerhardt would be in despair. Just the previous weekend he'd been caught in a raid on a male brothel in Elkton, Maryland, near the Aberdeen Proving Grounds, where military men were assigned. For all intents and purposes his career on TV was over.

Strange, though, Sean thought, that the man would come to an inn advertising open gay sexual activity as a choice of retreat from what he had experienced.

As Alex and he turned to see what possibly were their last guests slow down in a New Jersey plate car in front of the inn and then turn into the drive at the left of the inn that led to the parking area behind the building, Sean saw the young, small of stature, Hispanic waiter and room attendant, Ricky Sanchez, come out of the B&B, look around, and, upon seeing Allen Gerhardt, lean down and speak with him. Pulling himself out of the porch rocker, Gerhardt went into the inn with Ricky.

"Just had a dustup and a near thing in the kitchen with Val Thomas," Alex said, as he and Sean stood, looking at the business they were entering together.

"Flighty little thing," Sean said. "I'm not sure it was good to hire a transvestite."

"We agreed, I think, that we would have some variety around—for guests who wanted it. But there's a big problem with Val."

"What is?"

"She claims she's never been fucked. Keeping it a secret from us has made her shitty for days. She says she wants it, though. That she wouldn't have applied here otherwise."

"And so?"

"I will take care of that in my room at 10:00 tonight."

"Good. Might there be the same problem with Ricky?"

"No, I've fucked Sanchez three times already. He's a willing player. Randy little piece. I told him not to be forward with the guests, but he can be willing and he can keep any tips they give. I'll tell Val the same."

"Good," Sean said. "You know, I think this is going to work, Alex."

"Yeah, if we can keep the law off our tails."

"While you're doing Val in your room at 10:00 tonight, I have a session with Detective-Lieutenant

Pollack in the Anderson Cooper Media Room in the basement."

"So, we're not really going to keep the law off our tails. Taking one for the team?"

"It's a thick one too. And he wields it with anger."

"Thicker than mine?" Alex asked.

"Nope." They both laughed and turned their faces to the front door of the inn. Jeff Stockdon was hanging out of the door and waving to get their attention.

"I don't know." he whispered to them as the three walked down the hall from the foyer to the Tim Cook Office, where Jeff held sway. It was wedged between the Gore Vidal Dining Room running down the left side of the building, with the Michelangelo sunroom between it and the driveway, and Alex' kitchen on the back of the house. "He has two forms of ID, but I don't know. He looks pretty young and the guy he's with is controlling him really close. The little guy looks like he might cut and run if he has the chance."

Alex and Sean came up to a man with a much younger man and introduced themselves as the innkeepers as if they routinely did this for everyone.

The younger guy did seem close to underage to Sean and there was something about the demeanor of the two—a nervousness and a possessiveness on the part of the older man and a reluctance in the younger one—that was a bit disturbing. They were the last two of the arrivals for tonight, though, assigned to the Harvey Milk Room, located on the second floor, left, middle. It was one of the smallest guest rooms, with a double bed and a shower only. The man, Tom Miller, had booked it in his name and that of Andy Wilson. So, there was no subterfuge there. It was the age difference. But Wilson was of age according to his driver's license and his school ID.

There was a problem there—both IDs said he was nineteen, but the school ID was from a high school in

Trenton. In presenting it, though, the two were avoiding a challenge. There were nineteen-year-old students in high school. Ones who had been held back, sometimes to get another year of sports out of them, and though not tall, this young guy had an athletic build.

There was no question what they were here for. Miller had booked into an inn that had advertised only in gay media so far and as an anything goes place to stay. And he'd booked a room with one bed, a double, taking up nearly all of the floor space. He also was hugging the young man to him like he was afraid to give him room to run. But Andy Wilson, though trembling a bit and looking like a scared rabbit—as would seem natural in what Sean suspected was on here—was voluntarily sticking close to Miller.

They had no choice. They knew this possibility existed in their bookings, but the pair had all the right documentation.

Again, the three men, Alex, Sean, and Jeff, stood at the foot of the stairs and watched Tom Miller and Andy Wilson mount them.

And again, Jeff put his tongue in the side of his mouth and produced a loud popping sound.

"I think you're right this time, Jeff," Sean said.

"We should put in hidden cameras Jeff said," with a laugh. "I wouldn't mind seeing that cute little guy get his popped for the first time. Both have good bodies. Would be a lot of fun to watch. We could use the vid on the Internet for advertising."

"That isn't going to happen," Alex said. And he said it as more of a warning. This Jeff they'd hired for the front desk was a bit too slick. But he did have skills. In addition to everything else, he claimed to be a masseur. And Alex had already spied him fucking both Sean and Ricky and doing a flip-flop with Raif. Val was probably lucky that he didn't seem to like half and halves.

34

"Well, we're full up on our first night. Success so far," Sean proclaimed.

And seeming not to want to let it go, Jeff said, "And that honey that just walked up those stairs is gonna get filled up good tonight too. First first-timing in the inn and on the first night—maybe not even the night. The old man's probably sucking the young one off and fingering his ass already. Sure wish we had hidden cameras in those rooms."

"Go back to work, Jeff. There should be other reservations coming in to take care of." And turning to Sean and giving him a suggestive look, Alex said, "I think I could do with a siesta now that all of the guests have arrived. Then it's back to the kitchen to prepare for the morning."

As they walked down the hallway on the second floor toward the Christopher Isherwood Suite, Alex pushed his hand down the back of Sean's trousers and leaned over and whispered, "Thinking of that older guy spiking the younger one for the first time has made me horny."

"I could have guessed that," Sean answered.

Just to show Sean how strong and horny he was, Alex fucked him in his bathroom in what he called the Flying Spider position. Alex stood, feet flat on the floor, with Sean suspended in front of him, facing away from him, on the buried and thrusting cock. Alex was holding Sean's legs spread in front of him, with his hands grabbing Sean under the knees. Sean had his hands gripping Alex' hands, as Alex bounced Sean's ass on and off his cock to ejaculation.

Suggesting then that they go to their separate showers, Alex said he really did have to get back to work.

Sean was at the door to the suite to kiss him good-bye. "I really think it will work," he said.

"If I can fuck the snit out of Val before breakfast has to be served tomorrow," Alex said. "Which, of course, I can do," he added with a grin.

The Alexander the Great Suite

The candidate for the U.S. Senate, Martin Beardsley, was lying on his back on the bed in his bedroom, naked. He was groaning at the sensation of his campaign manager's cock rubbing against his. His hands were gripping the sides of young Derek Hillsman, who was straddling the candidate's pelvis, sheathing both cocks, and facing Beardsley's head. The palms of the young man's hands were pressed into the pecs of the candidate's hairy chest.

Hillsman's eyes were bugging out and his mouth was open in a big O. He was murmuring , "Oh, shit. Oh, fuck. Go easy," and "yes, yes, yes."

Beardsley's legs reached the floor at the base of the bed. They were spread and his black, hung campaign manager, Jock Johnson, was crouched between them, his hands on Derek's hips, his cock buried inside Derek's ass, stroking on top of Beardsley's shaft, which was remaining stationary. But Beardsley was feeling every stroke of Johnson's cock, and his moans were mingled with Hillsman's.

They were just about tired of this position and Johnson was showing his strategy smarts by formulating another one as soon as they'd made Derek come—which was within the next minute and a half.

The next position was much more satisfying to the long-time lovers, Beardsley and Johnson, and more athletic for all three of them. Derek was put into a Pile Driver position, his shoulder blades dug into the carpet at the base of the foot of the bed, and his legs jackknifed back over his shoulders. Facing each other at the end of the bed and standing over Derek's pelvis, both of the older men were able to work their cocks down and into Derek's now-gaping hole, while they embraced each other, kissed, and ran their hand over each other's bodies.

After a good ten minutes of this, Beardsley and Johnson didn't need Derek anymore. They left him in a panting heap at the base of the bed, and Johnson pushed Beardsley down on his stomach on the bed. Beardsley raised his pelvis to Johnson with a groan, and Johnson mounted his ass and fucked him to a mutual ejaculation.

Papers were strewn over the table in the sitting room. The men would get to them after the release of tension through sex and, by tomorrow, would have adjusted their campaign strategy for the next month. But priorities were priorities. Having been brave, sexually frustrated, and randy enough to book at this B&B, they'd be fucking in various configurations until suppertime.

The Front Porch

"You get all the stroke monitoring in you wanted?" Raif DuCorde walked half way up the side stairs to the front porch of GayLords and set the can of pink trim color down and laid the brush on top of it.

"Never can stroke enough," Sam Sterling, aka the rock star Snake, shot back, suspending the fingering of the guitar he held in his lap.

"I think you were watchin' every stroke of my brush."

"It wasn't your brushwork I was watching," Sterling answered. "Even in a paradise for men like this, you are eye candy for the soul."

"So, you like what you see, mon?" Raif said. "Like it as well at a closer look?" He came up on the porch and perched on the rail within three feet of where Sterling sat in a rocker.

Raif, in fact, was a feast for the eyes for a man who appreciated men. A rich chocolate brown, he was tall, handsome, and hard bodied, with a cascade of dreadlocks framing his face. And he didn't keep his body a secret. He was wearing a mesh athletic shirt that left nothing of the muscular, smooth milk-chocolate skin of his cut torso and six pack to the imagination. His silky basketball shorts were draped close to his thighs, and when he perched on the porch rail, his bulging basket was pushed out. He was half hard. He'd been keeping an eye on Sterling too, just in cut-off jeans shorts and also hard bodied, with a wiry build and a riot of tattoos, and he liked what he saw.

"I like it just fine," Sterling answered. "You're not an American black, are you? The Caribbean?"

"Jamaica, mon, where all men are handsome and hung."

"I can see you're handsome. You're hung too?"

"Better believe it, mon. So, you know, it says you are a Sam Sterling on the registration book, but I know who you really are. You're Snake. Love your music, dude, it makes me feel so . . . so . . ."

"Horny?"

"Yes, that's it, horny. We doin' some sort of mating dance here?"

"I am. I hope you are too. That's what I've come here for. I came here to fuck men."

"You come here to fuck or to be fucked?"

"Does it matter? You look fun loving. I go both ways, so there's no problem on my side."

"It's our lucky day, then, mon," Raif answered. "I swing too." He slid his right foot out of his sandal and nudged it between Sterling's thighs and under the guitar. Sterling pulled it into his crotch and massaged it as they talked and danced around where they both knew this was heading. "We gonna be fuckin' in a few minutes?"

"It appears that way."

"But you got woman fallin' all over you, mon. I've seen some of your concerts. You practically fuck them on stage. You sure you came to the right B&B?"

"I'm sure. It's all stage magic. Men throw their girlfriends on stage and I fool around with them for the cameras, but after the concert I take the boyfriends backstage and fuck them good. I come to places like this to recharge from what I have to do on stage. As you said, I'm here to fuck and be fucked. The more the merrier, the more manly the more satisfying, and the sooner the better."

Raif laughed and dug his heel into Sterling's crotch. "You take it rough, do you?"

"Do you take it rough?" Sterling answered, squeezing Raif's foot hard.

"You come to places like this incognito? What kind of name is Sam Sterling?"

"It's my real name. Snake is more of a description of me."

"Description of what, mon?"

"What do you think?"

"I'm wondering if you want to stay out on this porch or make good use of the Freddy Mercury Suite upstairs."

"They let the hired help cavort with the guests here?"

"They *encourage* the hired help to fuck with guests."

The Elton John Suite

Ricky Sanchez stood for a full minute without moving—without breathing either, just inside the door of the Elton John Suite that he'd gone to to check on whether Val had stocked it with towels. His eyes were bugging out at the sight of the pistol on the nightstand with the loose bullets beside it. Next to it were a three-quarters-empty bottle of whiskey and a glass from the bathroom. When he'd recovered his wits, he slid on by the wall into the bathroom, nonsensically checking the towel supply as he originally intended.

His mind was racing. He'd already made the connection between the guest registered to this room, Allen Gerhardt, the TV comedian, with the newspaper articles on the raid on the male brothel near the Aberdeen Proving grounds—or very likely had. That was thanks to Jeff Stockdon at the reception desk, who showed him two newspapers—one with a fuzzy photo of the raid in which that just might be the TV comedian in the background, but carrying no names, and another article listing an A. Gerhardt among the clients arrested at the site but not including any photos. Stockdon was good at ferreting out such information.

Ricky had volunteered to attend to the Elton John Suite when he'd first seen that the TV comedian, who Ricky rather fancied, was registered there. Val had said she had already put towels in the room, but Ricky thought the transvestite he shared a job and a room with was flighty, so he'd wanted to check the towel situation himself. He also was rather hoping he'd encounter Gerhardt in his room and maybe get something going. If it was the same Gerhardt who had been picked up in the brothel raid, that wasn't seen as a "bad thing" by Ricky. He fancied the man and wasn't above picking up some pay-for-sex money himself.

After all, what would a man check into this B&B for if it wasn't for a bit of sexual exercise?

But seeing that gun sitting there next to the bed and the bullets raised a whole different, disturbing reason the man was here. And his suitcase, closed tight, was on the luggage rack—like he didn't plan to use anything in it. Except for the pistol, maybe.

Ricky knew he should go directly to Sean or Alex, but then he'd never get to meet the man. And he did fancy him. He decided to go looking for him, eventually finding him sitting on the front porch of the B&B, looking depressed, and rocking in a chair absentmindedly.

"Mr. Gerhardt, you're in the Elton John Suite, aren't you?" Ricky continued without giving Gerhardt an opportunity to answer, and the TV comedian was too glazed over to respond immediately. "I'm the room attendant for your suite. There's something I need to show you to operate in your room. Would this be a convenient time? Can you come up the second floor for a few minutes?"

Gerhardt didn't demure. He stood in somewhat of a daze and turned to Ricky, who helped him through the door, into the foyer, and up the staircase. Gerhardt smiled wanly at Ricky, vaguely calling him a "pretty boy," and Ricky smiled back.

He was afraid to say that he enjoyed Gerhardt's TV work too much for fear of Gerhardt focusing on the seriousness of the situation he was in, but he couldn't help but say, "I think you are even more handsome than the TV shows you. I guess, though, that you can't look sexy, like you do now, on the programs you play in."

Gerhardt gave Ricky an appreciative smile, and, again, Ricky gave Gerhardt a "you can have me if you want smile." The ads in the underground media for this place had made pretty clear that the staff was available for the recreational comfort of the guests.

Ricky was working hard to have Gerhardt thinking of him as comfort rather than what he was afraid Gerhardt was contemplating. Ricky put an arm around Gerhardt to help him up the stairs, and Gerhardt put an arm around Ricky too, with one hand falling on—and remaining on—a butt cheek of the very-nicely-turned-out small Hispanic room attendant.

The depressed TV comedian noticed immediately upon entering the room that the pistol and bullets were missing. The whiskey bottle and glass were there, though.

"Where is . . . ?" He realized that he couldn't really ask where his gun was. There was no reason he should have a gun here, and he certainly didn't want to reveal why it *had* been here.

"I thought you might be more interested in something else here at the GayLords," Ricky said, pouring the man a glass of whiskey, handing it to him, and gently pressing him down to sitting on the side of his bed. Ricky gave him a provocative look, said, in a husky voice, "I've thought you were so sexy on TV that I've had dreams of you fucking me." He immediately went into a slow striptease for Gerhardt, followed by slow lap dance for him, followed by sitting in Gerhardt's lap, facing him, with his feet flat on the bedspread on either side of Gerhardt's thighs, his arms around Gerhardt, and his lips on Gerhardt's lips, and bouncing up and down on Gerhardt's hard cock.

As he hoped, he'd made Gerhardt forget all about his pistol, let alone using it.

For insurance, after Ricky had teased Gerhardt's load of cum out of him and told him how masterful he was, Ricky murmured, "I can come back after the dinner service to you—and even spend the night, if you wish."

Gerhardt did wish and he didn't ask again were his gun had gone.

When he left the room, Ricky took the pistol he'd hidden in the corridor straight to Sean, who understood the problem perfectly and told Ricky, by all means, to give Gerhardt special attention that night. Sean would see what he could do the next day to keep from having to clean up the splatter from the Elton John Suite and have it redecorated.

Much to Allen Gerhardt's comfort he and Ricky played Cowboy much of the night, with Ricky riding the man's cock to distraction—which was rather the point.

The Freddy Mercury Suite

The handyman, Raif DuCorde, and the rock star, Sam Sterling, were rolling around on the floor of the Freddy Mercury Suite, their clothes gone, thrown off to the side by one clawing what clothes there had been off the other. This process hadn't taken long. Sterling's tattooed body was wiry, but he was hard muscled. Raif, though, was heavier and more muscular. It wasn't an equal fight, and Sterling was horny enough not to prolong it.

It's just that neither had agreed to who got to fuck the other first. They were both in full erection, Sterling's shaft was long and thin, befitting the nickname Snake, and Raif's was thick, long, and jet black.

For minutes after Sterling had cried "uncle" and stopped struggling, Raif wrestled him, wearing him down to near exhaustion, so, when Raif rolled onto his back, and pulled Sterling's back over on top of him with arms laced under the rock star's armpits and holding Sterling's shoulder blades close into Raif's chest, and Raif raised and spread Sterling's thighs with his, and worked his thick, throbbing cock into Sterling's passage, Sterling just lay still, subdued. The victor, Raif, entered Sterling's passage with his cock and fucked him to an ejaculation.

Similarly, there was no struggle later when, standing against a wall with his legs spread, his buttocks thrust back, pulling on his cock, laughing, and letting his dreadlocks swirl around his head, Raif presented himself willing for Snake to grab his hips and fuck him deep from behind in long strokes.

They sat, cross-legged and facing each other on the bed afterward, trading sniffs of a bottle of poppers and

Sterling telling Raif of life on the road with a rock band and Raif impressing Sterling with tales of all of the rock band members he had fucked.

"In your travels, have you ever used these?" Sterling asked. He leaned over, opened the top drawer of the nightstand, and took out a black, leather-covered box. He opened it to reveal a series of graduated aluminum rods, or wands.

"Yeah, these are sounding rods. I've seen them in use before, but—"

"Don't worry, I don't want you to use them on yourself. I want you to put your cock in me and then fuck my dick with those rods. I cum unbelievably that way. Will you—?"

"Sure, why the fuck not?"

The two went into a Butterfly position, with Raif raised on his knees on the bed, his cock in to the root in Sterling's ass. Sterling's legs were spread over Raif's thighs, the heels of his feet pressed into Raif's buttocks. Sterling lay back, the bottle of poppers in his hand, going to his nose occasionally, and panting shallowly and groaning deeply, as one, after another, each rod thicker and longer than the previous one, Raif slowly and carefully inserted the rod into Sterling's piss slit, ran it down into the urethra canal, and slowly twirled it.

When Raif pulled the fourth rod out, Sterling arched his back, gave a little cry, and spouted cum all over Raif's chest and on his chin. Giving a laugh and licking his chin, Raif lowered his chest over Sterling's and pumped him hard and deep to Raif's ejaculation.

The Harvey Milk Room

2:30 p.m.: "You OK, so far, Andy? You did great."

"Yeah, I'm OK. It's fine, Coach." Andy Wilson murmured, belying the deer-in-the-headlights look on his face. The older, taller, and more muscular man, Tom Miller, leaned forward, licked cum off the young, classic blond nineteen-year-old slim but athletic-built Andy's cheeks and lips and shared it with the young man in a kiss. Miller was sitting on the bed, legs spread, with Andy kneeling between them. He had held Andy's curly blond head in his hands as he guided Andy in what to do.

"You sure you're OK? We could stop with that if you're not OK." He certainly didn't say it like he might be willing to stop.

"I'm fine, Coach. We're here. You went to a lot of trouble to be here. I'm sure you paid a lot for the room."

"I'm glad you appreciate how well I'm taking care of you, Andy."

3:15 p.m.: "There, it's done. There should be pleasure only from here. You did great. You OK, Andy? You OK with it? Cherry went pop, pop, pop. You're a man's man now."

"Yes, I'm OK, Coach." His voice was pained, and as if coming from far away—as if he's just coming out of a trance of blocking everything from his mind.

"Want you to be OK with it. It's better if you relax more, let it open to me. You do that, and it will be better next time. Such a sweet ass you've got. Really tight." Miller was standing between Andy's raised and spread legs, holding the ankles in his hands. Andy was on his back on the bed. The older man slowly let the young man's legs come down to a spread and bent position, his feet digging into the edge of the bed top. Miller leaned down over Andy's chest and took his mouth in a kiss.

Coming out of the kiss, Andy murmured, "Maybe we could . . . Oh, Coach. Oh, oh. Shit. Fuck!"

"Sorry, Andy, you're so sweet. Just this, once more, and then we'll rest. Yes, Yes, open up for me. You'll love it deeper! Ah . . . that's nice."

45

"There, that was better, wasn't it?" Miller whispered ten minutes later. "The extra lube helps." Miller hadn't said anything about condoms. He liked to deflower his virgins raw. "You still OK, Andy?"

"Yeah, Coach, I'm still good . . . just a little tired. Maybe we could . . ."

4:30 p.m.: "Oh shit, of fuck, fuck, fuck. I'm so sore. You're killin' me, Coach."

Andy was on his back on the bed, his buttocks at the foot edge of the bed. His arms were flung straight out from his body, his hands grabbing up gobs of the bedspread. Miller was standing below him, holding Andy's legs straight up, holding the young man's ankles together in a position Alex could have told him was a form of the Deep Stick. "Makes it really tight. Nice." His dick was in deep and he was rhythmically pumping Andy's ass and humming.

"You good, Andy? It good for you?"

"Yeah, it's good, Coach," Andy responded in a pain-edged voice. "This good for first squad on the soccer team, Coach?"

"Yeah, this very good, Andy. You're a star."

5:20 p.m.: "Open to me, baby. And cum for Daddy."

"Fuck me, Daddy."

Andy was on all fours on the bed, and Miller was crouched over his hips, fucking him fast, hard, and deep. He had one hand clutching one of Andy's pecs and the other was under the young man's belly, milking his cock.

"Yeah, open just like that. Jack off for Daddy. This is good, very good. You're going to be the team star."

6:15 p.m.: Sitting in the outdoor seating area of Hot Dog Tommy's on Jackson Street, just off Beach Avenue,

46

Andy sitting a little gingerly and chewing on his hot dog in a rather subdued manner.

"It's good with you, isn't it, Andy? It's what you wanted?"

"Yeah, Coach. It's good. It's what I wanted. When is the soccer roster coming out? Can I see where I'm posted on it before the list goes up?"

"I'm not sure that would be—"

"I'd like to see my name on the list—first squad—before it's posted." Andy's voice suddenly had a bit of a hard edge to it.

"Sure thing, Andy. We can do that. Eat up. I'm horny for it again."

Coming back into the B&B and headed to their second-floor room, they passed Val Thomas in the hall. She was dressed all in black, including her nails and lipstick. Despite her skirt over the tights and the falsies under her black T-shirt, it was unmistakable that she was a young man.

Interested and aroused, Coach Miller gave her a second look and an unmistakably interested smile. Blushing, Val lowered her head. The man was a hunk. She envied that young man he had his arm around, possessively, like the guy would cut and run if not held close. Val had stood outside the door, listening, from time to time during the afternoon. She was having trouble getting over the barrier herself, and here this young man was getting a real education. She had found herself moaning with him. God the man was a hunk. The blond was one lucky guy.

7:30 p.m.: The full Bully position, Miller standing in the middle of the room, legs spread and bent slightly. Andy was draped on his front, his torso held immobile by the coach having him in a full Nelson. Andy's legs were spread and hooked over Miller's slightly bent thighs.

Miller was bouncing Andy up and down, vigorously, on his cock, stroking the young man deep.

No holding back now. Fucking Andy totally.

"Oh, god, shit. Oh, god, fuck, Oh, god, shit!" was Andy's weak mantra.

Val was just outside the door, listening, in envy. Dreaming.

The Cole Porter Suite

Ted Landon was sitting in the tower sitting room off his bedroom, strumming on his guitar, searching for the next cord to go with the word in the lyrics he'd written that afternoon. He had showered and was in sleeping shorts. He'd tried to go to bed early after having walked the town and Beach Avenue in the afternoon, trying not to think of the e-mail he hadn't gotten. He hadn't been invited into the main draw of the U.S. Tennis Open. He'd have to go through the qualifying rounds to make it into the tournament. He knew his ranking had been going too far in the wrong direction.

But he hadn't had to go through the qualifying rounds in the last three years.

This obviously was a sign and had turned Ted to the song that had been bugging his mind. The lyrics just weren't setting in with the chords, and the melody just wasn't falling into place either. He was frustrated out of his mind. He wanted to move on from tennis, and song composing is where he wanted to move. He almost had; just not quite.

He rose to answer the knock on his door through the bedroom.

"Hi there, my name is—"

"I know who you are. You're Snake from the Catastrophic rock band. I saw that you were here."

"I heard what you're playing. Composing a song?"

"Trying to, but it isn't working." Ted had trouble taking his eyes off the riot of tattoos on the man's chest. Sterling, aka Snake, was just wearing baggy shorts and was barefoot. His hair was mussed and he looked half stoned, which he was. Ted liked the look. It was exotic compared to what he was used to. And, god damn, the man was a legend in the music field—the field Ted wanted to enter. And so sexy.

"Can I come in? I have some ideas on what could fix that melody and the lyric. Just one word might do it for the lyric."

"Sure, you can come in and try," Ted said, standing aside to let Sterling enter. "But I might be a lost cause."

"Oh, you're too much of a hunk to be a lost cause. I was at the French Open last year. I saw your match. You fought to the end. I like a man who finishes well. If I help you with the song, can I fuck you?"

Sure, Sterling was bald and direct. A rock star like him usually need only ask to get what he wanted. But it wasn't a stretch to ask. This was a gay-insistent B&B. It had made clear that it was a hook-up hotel, and here Ted was, by his own choice.

"You can fuck me whether or not you help me with the song," he said, picking up his guitar and taking it over to the bed.

Ten minutes and Sterling had given Ted the perfect word change in the lyric and the accompanying perfect chord.

Thirty minutes later, following mutual blow jobs, Ted, at his request, was receiving his second Elevated Splits of the day, with him doing the splits on top of the dresser, hands pressed into the dresser top in front of him, and the Snake fucking him deep from behind, milking his cock with one hand, and cupping his chin with the other and pulling his head back for a deep kiss.

It was Drag Queen Karaoke night at Phillip's Bar. This is what had drawn the business partners Mel Duncan and Jack Wilder to Cape May this weekend in the first place. They ate dinner at the Cabanas Beach Bar and Grill on the corner of Decatur and Beach Avenue. Both were wearing business suits, although Duncan had a small suitcase with him, and both were earnestly talking business over their dinner.

Mel was the managing partner of the Philadelphia law firm and Jack was its financial officer. Between them they made all decisions for the firm. They were as close as could be—closer than their spouses, who were sisters, and their friends could imagine. Over dinner they talked law and business, the quirks of their wife sisters, and the needs of their children as they approached college.

There was nothing that Mel and Jack didn't know about each other's business, lives, marital problems, and each other's bodies—what made them tick, what aroused them, what made them shoot their loads.

After dinner, Mel trembling with excitement, they made their way to Phillip's Bar. Jack sat at a table in the audience, infused with love and admiration, his hand on his basket, as Mel, in drag, stood at the mike and lip-synched to Judy Garland singing "Somewhere Over the Rainbow." Mel took third place. He even received a small trophy which, of course, couldn't be taken home. The two had a small pied-à-terra in Philadelphia, where they kept such mementoes and where Mel was free to dress as he pleased and Jack was free to fuck Mel in drag.

Jack took Mel from behind in front of a full-length mirror backing a dressing table in one of the changing rooms behind the stage at Phillip's Bar. Mel's dress was bunched up around his waist, and he was bent at the waist, palms pressed into the top of the dressing table, black-mesh stockinged legs spread, teetering on red stiletto heels, and watching the "lost in the fuck" expression on Jack's face as the man stood behind him, hands on Mel's hips, and fucked his ass.

As careful as the two always were to keep their secret a secret from the world, there was a little thrill in doing it here in a changing room where anyone could walk in on them at any time. Of course, this is why they came to places like Cape May to do their nightclubbing. There were appropriate nightclubs in Philadelphia, but they wouldn't chance it that close to home.

Afterward, both dressed in business suits again, they walked stiffly back to the GayLords Inn. Although they couldn't help touching hands in dark, otherwise deserted areas of the streets they walked, they studiously avoided contact when in the light. Resisting the urge keyed them both up, so that both were trembling and giving each other furtive, lustful looks as they mounted the front steps of the B&B.

In the Renée Richards Suite, they undressed each other with shaky hands, showered together, the two big men filling the shower, making closeness a necessity, both moaning and groaning as they soaped each other up and fondled each other's body parts.

In bed, they lay side by side, each stroking the cock of the other to an ejaculation, as they contemplated how good it was to be able to get away together like this—but also how complicated life was that they couldn't just live together as a couple—and, because they were lawyers, as the heat of having fucked earlier and been jacked off more recently wore off, they both drifted off to sleep thinking of problems and issues at work.

Don Lemon Room

The reclusive thirty-year-old Baltimore TV news anchor, Cory Townsend, took dinner at 6:00 p.m. at the

51

Martini Beach Bar and Restaurant at the corner of Decatur and Beach, just two blocks from the B&B. He looked nervously about him as he ate, scrutinizing the other patrons but doing so in a way that he thought he wasn't being observed. He wondered if here, in the restaurant, he was being followed, and he went to great pains to exhibit himself as not worrying about anything that the other diners noticed him and wondered what was worrying him. Luckily, none of them recognized him.

On the walk back to the inn in the twilight, he thought he heard footsteps, but when he turned—surreptitiously, he thought—there wasn't anyone around who he thought was out of place.

In his room he watched the 7:00 p.m. news from Baltimore, thinking that the temporary anchor they'd brought in for the weekend had botched his lines. But, of course, no one could do what Cory did—or had been doing. That was the nub of the problem, though—what he had been doing. He had developed a case of the nerves. He'd been told to take a break. He'd booked into GayLords with expectations. But now that he was here, he wasn't sure. Maybe man sex wouldn't calm him down. But maybe it would. He'd been using male brothels as a calming mechanism. But for now, he needed to take a shower and go to bed early.

It was dark in the room and he was stretched out on his belly, naked, his mind racing. The room was small, just with a shower bath, but it was not on the beaten track inside the inn. It was on the third floor overlooking the roof of the sun porch and the driveway. The light from the outside didn't reach into this area, so it was pitch dark in the room.

His mind was racing and he didn't hear the movement—and would have had no idea where it came from if he did. Nor would he have had much time to react and certainly not the strength to counter the weight of the

52

man who came down suddenly on his back, taking the wind out of Cory's sails.

He knew it was a man instantly, because he was naked, and Cory felt the man's erection already rubbing inside Cory's buttocks crack as the man got Cory's wrists strapped to the brass headboard overhead and had the blindfold and gag on him. Cory tried to kick with his legs, as the man ran a strap under the bed to bind Cory's ankles, with his legs spread, There was give in the tension of the strap, but no hope of escape.

Cory hyperventilated and whimpered as the man put him slightly on his knees so that his cock and balls could be pulled through his thighs for the man to suck and worry alternating with eating his ass out. With a deep groan, Cory ejaculated.

This was the signal for the man to mount his ass and fuck him hard. Cory lay there, helpless, and moaning. He was exhausted when the man was finished, whipped off the bindings, and melted away in the darkness.

Cory lay there, panting, for several minutes before turning onto his side with a grunt, smiling a small smile, and drifting off to sleep.

The Truman Capote Library (first floor, back, right)

Alex came out of the Christopher Isherwood suit on the third floor, having decided to check to make sure Val was finishing up the cheesy egg casseroles to pop into the oven first thing in the morning as the main course for the breakfast part of the bed and breakfast. He thought he might as well do a sweep through the halls and public rooms too to make sure everything was in order.

At the landing on the third floor, he met up with Raif, who was on his way up to his bedroom, The Diesel Washington Room, in the attic. He spoke quietly with Raif, telling him the swimming pool would need to be skimmed the next morning. Raif kept looking up the stairs toward the attic, so Alex took a peek in that direction too. He saw the figure of a man at the turn of the stairs but it was too much in shadow for him to know who it was. He released Raif, knowing he had an assignation with one of the guests, which was fine with Alex. He wouldn't bother checking the attic out then.

He did a turn of the halls on the third floor. He could tell that men were at it in the Alexander the Great suite, and he gave a little smile, wondering how the political candidate would like having his little weekend here spread across the news media. But then, he and Sean had decided that they would be totally discreet and would honor all of their guests' privacy even if there was a goldmine to be earned in judicious blackmail.

They would keep the guests' secrets and, thanks to Sean's sexual relationship with the police detective responsible for the historical area of the town, the police would keep the B&B's secrets.

He heard men in the throes of sex coming out of the Cole Porter Suite too. "The rock star has found the tennis pro," he thought. Good. He knew the tennis pro was trying to get into music. From the sound of it the music pro was getting into the tennis pro's ass. He also knew from personal knowledge gathered earlier in the day that the tennis player was a good lay.

Nothing much was going on on the second floor. The men there must be worn out, he thought. The rock star in the Freddy Mercury Suite obviously was on the third floor screwing the tennis pro. The Harvey Milk Room where the older guy had been popping the cherry of the young blond all afternoon and evening was quiet. They apparently were worn out. And the Elton John Suite was quiet too. The TV comedian and Ricky Sanchez were either taking a break or were sleeping like babies in each other's arms. Ricky was a good, sweet lay, Alex thought. The comedian, who was up to his ears in worry, was getting his money's worth in coming here for solace—at least for now.

On the first floor, Alex talked to Val briefly to make sure she was getting everything prepared for the morning. As he passed the Truman Capote Library, he saw that a light was on in a floor lamp across the room, and he went in to investigate.

"Uh, sorry, I didn't see you there," he said as he came in the room to see the young man curled up in the corner of a sofa by the floor lamp.

"Sorry, I'll go upstairs," Andy Wilson murmured, coming out of his curl and yawning.

"You don't have to leave the first floor if you don't want to. This floor is open to all of the guests all of the time."

"Uh, thanks," Andy said. He made no move to get up.

"Maybe you don't want to go back upstairs?"

Andy looked a little frightened. "I don't know."

"Is this not all that you wanted, Andy?" Alex asked. "Do you not want to stay here tonight—upstairs—in your room? With that older man?"

"It's been kind of intense," Andy said.

"Where do you live, Andy?"

"Trenton."

"Do you want me to drive you home?"

"I think so, yes," Andy said, giving Alex a little smile.

En route to Trenton, Andy gave Alex a "come on" look from across the front seat. "It's really nice of you to do this, Mr. Renard," he said. "You're a nice man . . . and a really good looking one—and so big. I bet you work out a lot."

"What is this, Andy? You're not too shy all of a sudden."

"It's just that I should owe you something for taking me home. And you're a big man. I like big men. Maybe you'd like something from me. Maybe you could find someplace to stop that's a little private."

"What do you want to do in private, Andy?"

"Well, I could give you a BJ, if you like."

"And maybe I could fuck you in the backseat of the car?" Alex asked, keeping his voice calm.

"Yeah, if you like. I bet you have a big one."

"That wasn't your first time, back there in the B&B, was it?" Alex said.

Andy looked away, out of the passenger door window.

"Why did you let Miller think that?"

"He's my soccer coach. I want to get on the first squad this coming year. He likes to fuck virgins. So, I gave him what he wanted. I was a virgin for him."

"And you'd like to be a virgin for me?"

"Yeah, sure. You're nice to take me home. And I think you're a hunk. Maybe you've got a big one."

"Would you like to stop at a motel, Andy?"

"Yeah, that would be great."

In a motel on the outskirts of Trenton, Alex fucked Andy six ways from Sunday, showing him some of the more challenging male Kama Sutra positions for two hours. In the Fusion position, Alex sat in the small sofa in the motel room and Andy hovered over him, reversed, with Alex' dick in him, Andy's feet on the sofa beside Alex' hips, and his arms under him, clutching Alex' thighs, as he rose and fell on the cock. In the Fire Hydrant, Andy was sideways to the bed, his left foot on the floor and his left arm propping pressed into the bed, holding his body in position. He was gripping Alex' neck with his right hand and Alex was holding up his right leg and pounding his ass. The Leg Glider was a modified doggy style with Andy on his belly, both of his legs bent back, with his

56

gripping his ankles, while, standing on the floor at the end of the bed, Alex gripped the young man's waist and fucked him in long, hard strokes.

It was obvious that Andy had done this before—a lot. He took it like a champ.

When Alex had come, he went into the bathroom for a few minutes to clean himself with a washcloth and then he was back in the room to pick up his clothes.

"That was fun," Andy said. He lay there, on his belly on the bed, his legs spread and an arm drooping over the side of the bed, the poster child for "boy have I been fucked." "And you do have a monster cock," he murmured in admiration. "What position should we do now?"

"That's it, Andy." I'll leave you taxi fare to get home from here in the morning. "I've got work to do; I'm going back to Cape May. I'll let your coach know you made it home OK."

Harvey Milk Room

Missing Andy, Tom Miller came out of the room, wearing just bikini briefs. Val was right that he had a great body.

Val also was right there in the hallway herself, having finished in the kitchen and on her way to her room.

Smiling broadly, Miller trapped her in the hallway and embraced her. She didn't struggle much. She enjoyed the kisses. She also enjoyed how Miller had managed to find her cock even with what she was wearing. And she didn't object to his whispered propositions. It was time she lost it—and Alex was going to take it in an hour or so anyway.

8:45 p.m.: "There, it's done. There should be pleasure only from here. You did great. You OK, sweetie? You OK with it?"

"Yes, I'm OK," Val murmured. God, it had hurt. But he said the first one would. The first one? Does he intend? "Oh fuck, oh shit. Mercy. Mercy!"

He turned her from the Missionary position to a side split without dislodging his cock, and began a slow pump again. What a sweet piece this was, he thought. And a virgin. He could tell. Two virgins in one day. Eureka!

9:45 p.m.: "You good, sweetie? It good for you?"

"Yes, yes," Val answered weakly.

"Open to me, baby. And cum for Daddy."

"Oh, god. Oh, god."

Val was on all fours on the bed, completely naked, no indication other than the nail polish, lipstick, and long, straight hair falling over her shoulders that she actually was a young man. Her cock wasn't big, but it was in evidence. Miller was crouched over her hips, fucking her fast, hard, and deep. He had one hand clutching one of Val's pecs and the other was under the transvestite's belly, milking her cock.

"Yeah, open just like that. Jack off for Daddy. This is good, very good. You're going to be OK. You're taking it great."

One thing that Val wasn't going to be ever again was a virgin.

Diesel Washington Room

Candidate Beardsley's media consultant, young Derek Hillsman, his body like that of a sleek racehorse, was crouched on Raif's bed, his torso raised a few inches off the bed with his elbows bent and supporting his upper body and his slightly raised knees supporting his lower body. His head was raised and he was crying out to the

58

headboard of Raif's bed, "Shit you're big. Big cock. Big black bull. Yes, yes, give it to me!"

Crouched over his hips, on his knees, his fists buried in the mattress beside the young man's waist, his dreadlocks flying. Raif was riding Derek's ass like a jockey in the home stretch at the Belmont Stakes. As they were cooling down from the race, rewarded by a shared ejaculation, and stretched out along each other's bodies', Raif whispered, "Look what I borrowed from the rock star downstairs."

"What is that? What's in the black case?"

Derek found out what was in the black case in short order. Raif held him close and captive with one arm and a leg thrown over Derek's legs, as, instructing the moaning and nearly sobbing young man that he must hold very, very still, Raif slowly buried the first of the sounding rods in the piss slit of Derek's erect and throbbing cock.

"Enough?" Raif asked when he pulled the first one out.

"I'll try another one," Derek answered with a half sob.

The Anderson Cooper Media Room (basement under the Oscar Wilde Parlor)

"Oh, yes, fuck me, fuck me, fuck. Hard, deep. Give me your cock! Give me your cum!"

The position wasn't challenging—a Doggy fuck over the arm of a recliner chair in a line of chairs facing a large TV screen, and the cock wasn't particularly notable in any dimension. But the stroking was hard, cruel, and vigorous. This was Detective-Lieutenant David Pollack, who controlled the day-to-day monitoring of the historical district of Cape May, and Sean and Alex knew they were dancing along the edge of their B&B being declared a male brothel.

So, to Sean at 10:00 that evening, the man who was mounted on his ass, his hand buried in the hair on the back of Sean's head and pulling on it, arching Sean's body back to him, while he slapped Sean's rump with the other hand and vigorously rode Sean's passage, the detective was the best master fucker he'd had in a month.

Luckily he was a fast shooter too and was happy with singles. By 10:30 p.m. he was out of there and Sean was headed up to his room in the Christopher Isherwood Suite following a busy opening day at the GayLords Inn.

The Jack Kerouac Billiards Room (Basement, under the Gore Vidal Dining Room)

It had been a close call. Jeff Stockdon had had to pull his guest into the Tennessee Wine Cellar under the kitchen to avoid colliding with the policeman, Pollack, going up the stairs, followed not long afterward by Sean Temple.

Jeff wasn't supposed to be there. He lived out. There was no reason for him to be there except that the effeminate young man he'd met at Phillip's bar that night, a gay establishment on the western outskirts of Cape May, had said he'd never been fucked on a pool table before.

There were a couple of blue-felted billiards tables in the Jack Kerouac Room.

The young piece writhing under Jeff had squeaked his full satisfaction with the pool table position, being kept reasonably silent by Jeff's hand over his mouth as, like Raif was doing with Derek Hillsman four flights up, Jeff played Jockey in riding his sleek young race horse's ass.

The Christopher Isherwood Suite

Alex arrived back at the B&B close to midnight. After checking the kitchen and finding that Val had everything set up for the morning, he mounted the stairs to the second floor. As he approached the door to the Christopher Isherwood Suite, he heard low sobs and found Val curled up on the floor by the door, naked, and holding her clothes.

After ascertaining what had happened to her—and even though she had acquiesced to it, if not the roughness of some of it—he carried her into the suite and settled her on a sofa in the sitting room between his room and Sean's. Then, saying he'd be back in a few minutes, he went around the hallway to the Harvey Milk Room, knocked on the door, and, when Tom Miller answered it, he punched Miller in the face, saying, "That's just for the way you take virgins. You've paid for breakfast tomorrow, but I want you out of here by 10:00 in the morning."

Then, without looking back he went back to his suite. He didn't feel like sleep alone tonight. He went to Sean's door and opened it a crack.

Yet another Jockey race fuck was in progress. His brother, Eddie, was covering Sean and riding him hard to the finish line. He even had a riding crop and was putting it, albeit lightly, into play on Sean's ass.

Quietly shutting the door, he went to the sofa where Val was lying, leaned over, and scooped her up. "I've changed my mind," said to her. "I've decided you'll sleep in my bed rather than out here on the sofa." He took her into his room, laid her on the bed—and then laid her like a virgin really should be laid for the first time.

Cole Porter Suite

Raif stood outside the door of the Cole Porter Suite, listening for signs of wakefulness within. He could hear Ted Landon moaning softly and Sam Sterling humming quietly. Raif used his master key to enter the suite.

Sterling was sitting on the bed, cross-legged. Landon was sitting in his lap, his shoulder blades pressed into Sterling's chest. Landon's head was nestled into the hollow of Sterling's shoulder, and Snake held a open bottle of poppers to Landon's nose. With his other hand, Sterling was slowly twirling the third smallest sounding rod in Landon's urethral canal.

Seeing Raif enter, the tennis pro languidly opened his arms in welcome.

Ten minutes later, Raif and Sterling were pelvis to pelvis, facing each other. Raif was sitting up, Sterling was laying back, his hands gripping Landon's waist. Landon, facing Raif, was sandwiched between them, sitting on and sheathing in his passage both cocks—Landon taking both cocks at once, which he occasionally did with other tennis players on the circuit. Raif was holding Landon's erect cock steady with one hand, while he was bottoming and twirling a sounding rod in the cock with the fingers of the other hand. Landon was taking the sixth progressively larger sounding rod.

Raif pulled the rod out, and Landon, eyes glazed over from the effect of the poppers, gave a little cry and creamed Raif's belly. With a low laugh, Raif reached for the seventh sounding rod. Landon whimpered in the realization that Raif intended seeing how thick a rod Landon was able to take.

From the effect of the poppers and the excitement, Landon didn't go soft after ejaculating, and he could feel that there was more down there to come up. He was in ecstasy. He'd been sounded before but never above the fourth smallest rod. As the seventh rod came out, Landon's cock burbled out with more cum. Raif reached for rod number eight. A rhapsody of music was wafting through Landon's brain, lyrics and chords dropping like rain.

Derek Hillsman was stretched over the body of Martin Beardsley in a sixty-nine position on Beardsley's bed. Jock Johnson was kneeling behind Derek's spread legs, his hands grasping Derek's hips, his cock fucking Derek's ass. In a three-way fuck and suck, Beardsley was sucking Derek, Derek was sucking Beardsley, and Johnson was fucking Derek.

They all came within a fairly short period of time, and Derek rolled out from between the two older men, as Beardsley and Johnson went into a full-stretch embrace.

Within minutes the snoring of the three men joined that of most of the satiated and exhausted men through the mansion.

Chapter Three: Day Two, Sunday

Don Lemon Room, 3:00 a.m.

All was quiet across the GayLords Inn for nearly two hours. Most were asleep, sleeping the sleep of the well fucked. Cory Townsend was awake and trembling in hopeful anticipation, though. He was on his back, naked, his cock begging for the attention he himself couldn't give it, his eyes peering at the ceiling but not seeing.

He had heard some rustling—or maybe not—when the blindfold was slipped on his face and his wrists were seized and bound together. He lay there, whimpering and not resisting, as his ankles were bound as well. Strong hands turned him cross-wise in the bed, so that his head arched back over the side. The hands grabbed his head on each side, the thumbs stroking his cheeks.

Understanding and aroused, Cory opened his mouth in a big O. He shuddered and gagged as the thick cock entered his mouth and slid to the back of his throat. But within seconds he had adjusted to the stroking of the cock in his mouth and settled down to the face fuck.

Ten minutes later, he was on his back at the edge of the bed, his bound legs raising up a hardbodied chest, a thick cock stroking in his tight ass passage.

"Yes, yes, fuck me. Mine my ass deep," he murmured, and then, "Oh, my God, I'm gonna come. I'm gonna come." And then he did, in a shot that arced up, reaching his face.

Maintaining the hold on Cory's legs, the assaulting stranger continued stroking inside him.

Elton John Suite, 4:00 a.m.

Al Gerhardt moaned in his sleep and began to mutter. His body was shuddering. Ricky Sanchez could tell that Gerhardt was dreaming of the nightmare he was living in having been arrested at the male brothel near the Aberdeen Proving Grounds. Turning onto his back and nestling his buttocks into Gerhardt's groin, Ricky reached back, stroked Gerhardt's cock hard, and then positioned the bulb at his entrance. He moved Gerhardt's bulb around on the rim of his hole.

Snorting softly, but not waking, and no longer muttering, Gerhardt moved an arm over Ricky's chest and pulled him closer. Instinctively pushing his pelvis forward, Gerhardt's cock entered Ricky's passage. Sighing, Ricky turned his face to Gerhardt as the older man, still asleep but instinctively knowing he was inside Ricky and beginning to slowly stroke and move deeper inside him, returned Ricky's kiss.

Gerhardt was calm once more, and Ricky was sighing from the rubbing of the cock head on his prostate. He reached down and slowly stroked his cock to an ejaculation before drifting back off to sleep.

Christopher Isherwood Suite, 4:20 a.m.

Sean woke from the sound of the door from the suite's sitting room into the hallway quietly closing and the sound of Val's voice.

He was lying on his back on top of Eddie, who also was on his back, their heads nestled against each other, Sean's back arched, one of Eddie's beefy arms laying across Sean's chest, holding him close, and Eddie's cock, flaccid, inside Sean's passage.

Eddie grunted and snuffled as Sean pulled out from under him and rolled off the side of the bed on his feet, but the big man didn't wake. Sean padded to his bathroom; examined the evidence of welts on his flanks, which weren't too bad; showered; toweled off; and put a silken robe over his naked body. Inserting his feet into slippers, he went out to the sitting room. He checked Alex' room. It was empty, but the sheets on the bed were all messed up like someone had conducted a battle in there.

He went down to the kitchen, where he found both Alex and Val working on the breakfast, which would start service at 8:00 a.m., this being a Sunday. Alex looked pleased with himself and Val was humming as she moved around, giving worshipful glances to Alex from time to time, and touching him as she passed him.

"So you took care of the little joining our world problem?" Sean asked Alex.

"Yep," Alex answered.

"Yep," Val said, piping up and giggling.

"I'll take two cups of coffee, please," Sean said. "To go."

"Eddie still up there in your bed?" Alex asked.

"Yes, he is."

"Fucked you good, did he?"

"Yes, he did. That OK with you?" Sean half hoped that Alex wouldn't like his brother coming around and fucking Sean. Sean wasn't too sure about the introduction of the riding crop himself, although it had been used lightly.

"Fine. He a better fucker than I am?"

66

"You know I'm not going to answer that," Sean said, with a laugh. "You both are quite adequate," he added as he headed for the kitchen door with the two cups of coffee on a tray.

When he got to the room, Eddie was propped up on pillows against the headboard. His legs were spread and bent. He had a cigarette in one hand and had worked his cock up into a raging erection with the other.

"I brought coffee," Sean said.

"Put it down somewhere and come here," Eddie growled.

Eddie fucked Sean in a Lap Dance position, with Sean on the cock, almost sideways, facing away from Eddie and his legs bent and leveraging the fuck off the soles of his feet. One arm was slung around Eddie's neck, and his was beating himself off with the other hand as Eddie clutched and squeeze one of his butt cheeks, spreading it to give his cock deeper access to Sean's passage. The two kissed passionately as Sean rose and fell on the cock.

As they came out of the kiss, Eddie asked, "You just been with Alex?"

"He's in the kitchen, getting breakfast ready. With Val. I just got coffee and returned."

"Did he fuck you yesterday?"

"Yes."

"He fuck you better than I do?"

Brotherly rivalry never goes away, Sean thought. "You know I'm not going to answer that. You both are more than adequate."

Eddie scooted down in the bed, pulling Sean's shoulder blades into his chest in the close Pearly Gates position they'd been in when Sean woke up. The big man took over the stroking, thrusting as deep and as hard into Sean's passage as he could—taking over full control of the fuck, and maybe, just maybe, competing with his brother for master fucker number one with Sean.

The coffee got too cold to drink before Eddie had finished Sean.

The Alexander the Great Suite, 6:00 a.m.

Derek Hillsman came awake with Martin Beardsley sucking his cock and Jock Johnson fingering his ass open. Before he was fully awake, he was sitting on Beardsley cock, facing Beardsley's feet, Beardsley on his back and holding Derek's waist in his hands, and Jock Johnson, erection in hand, was moving in on his knees, over Beardsley's stretched legs, and toward Derek's pelvis.

Beardsley moved an arm around Derek's torso under his pecs and pulled the young man's shoulder blades back into this chest, rolling Derek's pelvis up. Johnson grasped Derek's ankles, hooked them on his shoulders, and continued sliding up into Derek's groin. Derek cried out and Beardsley jerked and started panting hard, as Johnson's cock started sliding into Derek's passage in a Double Penetration fuck above Beardsley's buried cock inside Derek. Johnson threw an arm around Derek's neck to bring him in for a deep kiss and encased Derek's cock with his other hand as he started stroking his cock inside Derek and rubbing it against the already-encased cock of Beardsley.

"Just a quickie before breakfast," Johnson had whispered before possessing Derek's mouth and started to pump him.

The Gore Vidal Dining Room, 8:30 a.m.

Nearly all of the guests, most of them looking a bit hung over, were in the dining room for breakfast, as Ricky and Val moved around the tables, serving the men. Sean

68

stood in the doorway between the dining room and the foyer, supervising and listening for the expected ring at the front door.

Martin Beardsley, Jock Johnson, and Derek Hillsman were at one table. The two older men were talking politics with great animation and were snarfing up food like their fuel tanks were running on empty. Derek Hillsman was nodding his head at appropriate moments, but he looked subdued and overtired.

Sam Sterling and Ted Landon were sitting at another table, Ted all smiles and humming notes and trying out lyrics with wide gestures. Sterling was sitting there with a knowing look on his face.

"All this inspiration is from Raif and me fucking your cock with those rods, you know," he said in a low voice, leaning over the table.

"Do you think so?" Landon said, startled by the suggestion.

"Eat up your breakfast and let's go to my room," Sterling said.

Landon started to gobble up his food.

Sean's focus turned to the politico table, where Beardsley and Johnson were now arguing. Hillsman was trying to intervene, but not having much success. Whatever the two men were arguing about, the altercation had turned vicious, by the looks on their faces, although the vocal level had been kept to a hush. Beardsley suddenly threw his napkin down and stalked out of the room. After a moment of a hissing exchange between Johnson and Hillsman, Derek said, "Well, I'm going to the library to check out the overnight political news until the two of you cool down." Johnson left then, clumping out of the room and up the staircase in the wake of Beardsley.

Allen Gerhardt was at another table, alone, and lost in his thoughts and worries, barely touching his food. Mel Duncan and Jack Wilder were also at separate tables, studiously ignoring each other, but each with a knowing little smile on his face. Sean smiled and shook his head when he glanced at them, even faced away from each other at their separate tables. Who did they think they were fooling? he thought. But beyond being amused he didn't care. They had paid for their fantasy and respect for their secret. And they would likely be return guests.

Tom Miller, a Band-Aid on his nose and what looked like a black eye forming, sat quietly, face down, eating quickly, at another table. Whenever Val passed by the table, he'd look up and give her a little sneery smile. At first she didn't look at him when she passed, but increasingly she found a reason to pass him by, and eventually she was giving him little smiles too. Alex had handled her masterfully last night, but there was something about the intensity of Tom Miller. He had fucked her first, and roughly at times, but he was a hunk and a half, and he'd fucked her first, been the first to fulfill the fantasies she'd had for some time.

Cory Townsend didn't appear for breakfast. He'd called down to have it brought up to his room to him. Alex had called Raif into the kitchen to do that, as Ricky and Val were busy in the dining room. Ricky was spending as much of his time as possible making sure Allen Gerhardt was OK and didn't need anything.

Alex appeared at the door from the kitchen to survey how breakfast was going, everyone having been served now. He gave Miller a scorching look that made the soccer coach turn his head away. Alex scowled again when he looked across the room to see that his brother, Eddie, the charter boat captain, was at a table and had been served double portions of everything. Alex had taken note of the telephone number of the young boat crew member Eddie had brought home to fuck the night Alex and Sean had won the bid for this inn—the nice little piece Alex had fucked while Eddie was fucking Sean

70

upstairs. Alex would have to track the guy down and fuck his lights out just as a response to Eddie showing up here occasionally, nailing Sean all night, and then expecting special coffee and breakfast service.

From time to time in the night Alex' mind had gone to the riding crop he'd seen Eddie using on Sean. If Sean liked that sort of shit, he thought, Sean wasn't as much the man for him as Alex had thought he was.

The service was complete, but diners were still eating when the front door bell rang and Sean answered it. The man at the door introduced himself; he had been expected. Sean escorted him into the dining room and over to Gerhardt's table, excusing himself and backing away when Allen Gerhardt saw his brother, Averett.

"Averett. What are you doing here?"

"I came for you, Allen."

"All the way from Indiana?"

"It's far enough away from here that I think it best you come live with Marianne and me for a spell. This will all die down. You can recover from this."

"But Marianne . . ."

"She's good with it. We're not living in the nineteenth century. None of it is a surprise to us, and we don't think any differently about you just because you are in trouble over it. Come on, Allen. The car's just outside."

As soon as Averett had arrived in the dining room, Ricky had gone up to Gerhardt's room, packed the man's bag, and was bringing it downstairs when the Gerhardt brothers entered the foyer.

"Just a minute," Allen said. "Let me talk to this young man a moment." He drew Ricky into the music room, pulled the young man to him, and kissed him passionately on the lips. "Thank you; you saved my life," he said. "I know what you kept me from doing." He pulled a couple of hundred-dollar bills out of his pocket and pressed them into Ricky's hand.

"No, I can't accept this. I wanted to be with you."

"Thank you for saying that, but I know if you hadn't taken the pistol away and stayed with me—and probably had a great deal to do with my brother being here to get me—I'd be a dead man now. And making love to you yesterday and this morning has convinced me I don't want to die. My cell phone number is there too. If you want to, please call me. I'd like that. You were the sweetest lay I've ever had."

Ricky walked back with him to the front door and stood on the front porch as the Gerhardt brothers got into Averett's car. Ricky didn't notice the sound of several motorcycle motors until the car was pulling away. He looked up at the black-leather-clad motorcycle gang idling on their bikes across the street and a couple of them looked back at him. They were Hispanics. Recognition hit both sides of the street at the same time. With an "Oh, shit," Ricky backed through the front door, turned and hurried to the back of the building.

A couple of the gang members started to get off their cycles, but just then a police car pulled up to in front of the inn and two men got out, both in suits, both obviously cops.

Sean answered the door. "David," he said, seeing Detective-Lieutenant Pollack standing there with a man Sean didn't recognize. "What can I do for you two?" Sean asked, clearly surprised, as Pollack should have been well bribed into the next month.

"This here's Detective Peter Randal from the Trenton police," Pollack said. "You got a guest here named Tom Miller? He's wanted for questioning in Trenton. Several parents have signed complaints over sexual matters he is connected with as a coach."

"Yes, he should be in the dining room," Sean said, not the least bit surprised that Miller might be in trouble in Trenton over conduct with his soccer team players.

But Miller wasn't in the dining room anymore.

Harvey Milk Room, 8:45 a.m.

Tom Miller was standing in the middle of his room, his suitcase open on his bed and nearly packed. He was performing a full Bully fuck on a naked Val, suspending the smaller body of the transvestite in front of him, pinned by his buried cock, Miller's arms holding Val's torso to his by running up the young transvestite's body and grasping her head between his hands. Miller's thighs were slightly bent and Val's thighs were laying over them.

Val was in seventh heaven and squeaking her delight. Her first man was inside her again.

It took the two cops and Alex to pry them apart, and, as the cops were leading Miller off, Val was sobbing, trapped in Alex' arms, and trying to reach for Miller again.

"You want a Bully fuck, I'll give you a Bully fuck," Alex muttered, hauling Val down the hall to the Christopher Isherwood Suite and performing not only a completed Bully on her but a Bodyguard as well, fucking her behind while palming her breasts and kissing he hollow of her neck. He followed this up with a Bent Spoons, Val lying on top of Alex on the bed, with Alex grabbing underneath her thighs and raising and spreading them while vigorously fucking her channel.

Afterward Val was purring and blowing bubbles and already beginning to forget all about the soccer coach who had popped her cherry.

The Don Lemon Room, 8:50 a.m.

The tray of food Raif was taking to Cory Townsend was dumped out on the floor near the door.

Raif was fucking Cory in Bumper Cars position, Cory's legs on the bed but his torso streaming down toward the floor with him on his elbows, his cheek pressed to the carpet. Reversed on him and headed in the other direction, Raif was leveraging off the balls of his feet on the floor on either side of Cory's body. He was grasping Cory's ankles, Raif's dreadlocks whirling about his head, as he took the young TV anchor's ass in vigorous, hard, reverse thrusts.

Townsend cried out the vigorous assault on his body with cries of "Yes, yes, fuck me. Fuck me hard," exhilarated by the knowledge that the cock pounding his ass was the same one he'd had twice in the dark already.

Freddy Mercury Suite, 8:50 a.m.

Sam Sterling was holding Ted Landon close in his arms. The two were murmuring rhythms and humming musical runs to each other, as Sterling held Landon's erection steady with one hand and twirled a number four rod in his piss slit with the fingers of the other hand.

Foyer, 9:00 a.m.

Sean was watching Tom Miller being loaded into the police car as a cowboy type, long and lanky, was walking up the steps. Every inch the cowboy, he was wearing tight jeans, a flannel shirt, a cowboy hat, and boots. If he'd been chewing on a wheat stalk, he couldn't have been more the Texas cowboy.

"Howdy," he said, as he mounted the porch steps. "Might you be the proprietor of this inn? My name's Tex. Don't have a reservation but wonder if you might have a room for a night or two."

Of course your name is Tex, Sean thought. Then thinking of the room Miller had just been pulled out of, he said, "Yes, if you can wait for us to clean the room, we've just had a vacancy. If you'll go on through to the office, our receptionist, Jeff Stockdon, will get you registered."

"Ricky, Ricky," Sean called out at the dining room door once Tex had walked back toward the office. "We need the Harvey Milk Room redone right away, please."

But Ricky wasn't in the dining room or the kitchen.

No one else was in the kitchen now either. Alex had Val upstairs readjusting her attitude about Tom Miller.

The kitchen door to the parking area and dumpsters was open.

The Parking area, 9:00 a.m.

The third Hispanic motorcycle gang member was taking his turn mounted on Ricky's hips and gang fucking the young man they'd pulled behind the dumpster when he took the trash out back and beat him down before they started fucking him.

A tough young man, he had taken the beating and was taking the fucking without imploding. He'd been in a gang himself—one that had rumbled with this one. They were getting their own back on him.

Then Sean was coming out the back door, screaming bloody murder. He was backed up by an appreciably larger Eddie wielding his riding crop. The gang members hopped off Ricky and ran for their bikes at the end of the alley and roared off.

"Are you OK?" Sean asked, crouching down beside Ricky's prone body.

"I'll be OK," Ricky said, blood streaming down from his mouth.

"You won't be OK for the rest of this day," Sean said. "Let's get him upstairs to his room, Eddie." Sean motioned for Eddie's help in giving Ricky support to stand up.

75

"They took my money," Ricky was mumbling. "He just gave it to me and they took it."

"They left your life, Ricky. That's what's important. But no more work for you today." Running through Sean's mind was whether their backup room attendant, Brad Taggert, was available on such short notice. The inn was full. They couldn't run on just flighty Val in the dining room and attending the suites.

Tim Cook Office, 10:00 a.m.

Sean came to the B&B office to call the doctor to attend to Ricky and then Brad Taggert to see if he could come in and work as a waiter and room attendant while Ricky was recovering from the injuries he sustained out behind the dumpster. Sean was a bit irritated that Jeff Stockdon, the reception clerk, wasn't at the office, but when he saw that the register book was missing, he remembered that Jeff had set up shop out at the pool house, because he was giving full-body massages out there today.

Hanging up from the call to Doctor Claude Overby, Sean saw the corner of the second book of registrations—the one with the "cover" names in it—peeking out of the shelf under the reception counter, and he pushed that back under while he picked up the telephone.

Arriving just then, though, suitcase in hand, and a somewhat forlorn look on his face, was one of the lawyers from the back of the top floor, Jack Wilder.

"Are you checking out early, Mr. Wilder? Are you not enjoying your stay?"

"Yes, I have to check out. Duty calls. I have to be in the office early tomorrow," Wilder answered. "But I had a wonderful time."

"I hope you did," Sean said, and he couldn't help but adding, "We are completely at your service here. There is no way you can exercise your preferences here that we will not fully support. I hope you understand that and will come back whenever—and with whoever—you desire in the future."

Perking up a bit, Wilder shook Sean's hand and said, "Thank you, thank you very much. I certainly will be back."

"And when you come back and if you bring someone, feel free to book only one room, if you'd like to be together," Sean said. "We fully understand. And, for your information, our registrations are set up to give our guests complete privacy and deniability."

Wilder left the B&B standing taller and with more of a smile on his face than when he'd come to check out.

Sean wanted to assure him that he and Mel Duncan didn't have to space their departures or any other movements to camouflage why they had been here and that they'd been together. But he felt he had gone about as far as he could to assure the two lawyers that they could come here and be what they wanted to be to each other with zero hassle.

That done, he picked up the phone. Time to try to enlist Brad Taggert. The young man was a bit of a loose cannon but he was experienced—quite experienced—in Sean's knowledge, although Alex hadn't vetted him yet and would have to, and there was the advantage that he was fully versatile in his servicing ability.

Phillip's Bar, 10:15 a.m.

Brad Taggert, twenty-two, muscular, blond, and a bit thuggish looking that spoke of experience and a bit of rough to many men, padded out to the main bar at Phillip's to answer the phone. He had hastily pulled on his jeans when he'd heard the call up the corridor that he was needed on the phone. En route, he'd grabbed a packet of cigarettes and was lighting up.

Back in the dressing room he'd left, the middle-aged transvestite he'd been fucking on a studio couch was still moaning her pleasure, lying on her back, her dress bunched up around her stomach, and her wig on the floor next to the couch, having come off in the struggle of getting Brad's cock inside her and pumping her hard. Her legs were open and spread, her ankles turned on the outer edges of the couch, as she hadn't managed to keep the stiletto heels of her red spike shoes flat on the bed as Brad was pounding her.

Brad regularly had rentboy duties at the bar on weekend mornings—using his ability and willingness to go both ways. That meant the bar only needed one guy available on a Sunday morning. There rarely was any demand on a Sunday morning. A bit more on a Saturday morning.

Some twenty minutes earlier, Brad had come into the bar from the back and was surprised to see the transvestite there—recognizing her from the drag queen Karaoke contest from the previous night. She was middle-aged but tricked out pretty good for a drag queen. She was wearing the same dress, black mesh stockings, and red spike heels as the previous night. She also looked sad and had sunk into her beer.

"You look like you've lost your best friend, honey," Brad sad, saddling up to the stool beside Mel Duncan.

"I feel like I have—at least for now. This weekend was Disneyland; tomorrow begins reality again."

"You were here with a man last night. He desert you?"

"He had to leave. He hasn't deserted me, though. He just took all of the joy and fun of the weekend with him when he had to go."

Brad put a hand on Mel's back, rewarded by a slight shudder and Mel turning his face to the young man and giving him a wan smile.

"Fancy a young man's cock for $50?" Brad asked. "We can extend that weekend of magic for another half hour."

Forty-five minutes later, emerging from the back to answer the phone, Brad perked up. The prospect of some steady employment for a few days. "Sure, I can do that. Any action at the inn?"

"More than you can imagine," Sean answered. "You'd have to be vetted by Alex Renard first, of course—not the waiter or room attendant part; the servicing part."

"No problemo," Brad answered. "You want me to come right over now. Again, no problemo."

Sean disconnected the phone, only worrying now about where they could free a room to assign Brad. It probably would have to be one of the smaller guest rooms. Unlike Ricky and Val, but very much like Raif, Sean expected Brad to need a room to himself where he could service guests if they didn't want to use their own rooms. Brad was a player.

The Chris Steele Room, 10:45 a.m.

Ricky Sanchez was on his back on his bed, groaning. He'd been patched up from his attack by the members of a rival Hispanic motorcycle gang, but there was a new reason to be groaning. A older man, a bit heavy set, but not disgustingly so, was pulled up on a chair close to and facing the side of the bed. He was fully clothed other than his fly being open and his dick out. His dick was particularly exposed, though, as Ricky was twisted in the bed so that he could have the dick in his mouth and the older man could have his film-covered hand inside Ricky's ass up to his knuckles.

The older man was twisted around so that the left hand was crammed up Ricky's ass and the right was stroking Ricky's erect cock.

"Give it to me, son," the man was murmuring. "Relax and just release it." The fingers of the hand inside Ricky's ass were expertly stroking Ricky's prostate, so it wasn't long before Ricky gave the man what he was asking for—Ricky exploded in an ejaculation.

That, of course, wasn't the only thing the man wanted. He leaned back in the chair with a sigh, as Ricky sucked his cock to a tonsil-creaming finish.

Sean waited just outside the open door for Dr. Overby to finish patching Ricky up and taking his partial payment for the house call.

Christopher Isherwood Suite, Alex' Room, 10:45 a.m.

Alex, resting in his room between cleaning up from the breakfast service and starting work on the B&B's first open dining service for the supper hour, woke with a snort to find a hard, but sexy-looking young blond crouched over his pelvis and deep-throating his cock.

The young man was so good at blow jobs and Alex so far along in his throbbing erection and rising sap and jaded in his sexual experience and expectations that he just laid back, threw an arm over his face, and groaned his way through ten minutes of cock and balls sucking and ass finger play. He didn't know who this guy was, and he didn't care who this guy was as long as he kept using his hands and soft mouth as expertly as he did.

Sensing that Alex was about to come and wanting to hold him off, the young man took his mouth off the cock, held it steady so that Alex' urge would subside enough not to cause an eruption, and turned his rugged, handsome face up to where their eyes could meet as Alex moved his forearm off his face.

"I'm Brad Taggert," the young man said. "Mr. Temple has brought me in as a substitute for Ricky Sanchez. He said I'd have to pass inspection with you first, though."

Alex grunted. "The services here require more than blow jobs."

"I understand that," Brad said. "Just stay there, like that. Come when you want to."

Rising up over Alex' naked body, Brad saddled himself on Alex' pelvis, held Alex' cock steady with a hand, as the young blond easily swallowed the cock down to the root in his ass channel. Showing off his expertise, Brad started the fuck on Alex' cock with a Cowboy Splits, his legs straight out from his body in the splits, leaning his torso down into Alex', with their lips meeting, Alex embracing his torso and, his legs spread, thrusting up into Brad's ass. Brad then moved to a Cowboy Sideways, with his body sideways to Alex' and Alex holding him inches off his body with his left arm holding Brad's legs together in an embrace, and his other arm supporting Brad's back, with Alex palming one of the young man's pecs. This position gave Alex a couple of inches of thrust space in stroking his cock up into the young man's ass.

Then, moving to a Cowboy Reverse, Brad rode the cock like a rodeo star. Suddenly fully awake, holding the young man's waist in his hands and yodeling his approval of the ride, Alex took fifteen minutes of vigorous, athletic, exciting ride to shoot his load.

Brad arched his back down to Alex' chest, laying his cheek against Alex', and, Alex enclosing Brad's torso in his two close-embracing arms, the two kissed and murmured how good the fuck had been. All the time Brad was slowly moving his hips, caressing the cock inside him, with quickly took the hint and reengorged.

Brad threw his shoulder blades back into Alex' chest, wrapped his arms around Alex' neck, and Alex grabbed the flexible young man's thighs and held them raised and straight out from his body, while Alex fucked hard up into to a second ejaculation in a variation of his favorite Pearly Gates position.

Cooling down afterward in the same position but with Brad's legs lowered and bent and feet on the bed on either side of Alex' thighs, Brad whispered, "Did I pass the audition?"

"You sure as hell did. But how did you know to end in a Pearly Gates?"

"You are a legend at Phillip's bar—as are your preferences."

"Can you fuck a man as flexibly and inventively?"

"Want to take my cock?"

"That's OK. We'll try you out on an interested guest."

"How about your partner, Mr. Renard."

"We'll try you out on an interested guest."

Christopher Isherwood Suite, Sitting Room and Sean's Room, 11:00 a.m.

"I'm so grateful you will make house calls, Doctor," Sean said in a low voice, as Dr. Overby came out into the hall and closed the door to the Chris Steele Room. He looked at the plaque next to the door. "The Chris Steele Room?" he asked.

"One of my favorite gay porn stars," Sean exclaimed.

"Ah. You know I won't mind making house calls here—considering the method of payment."

"Ah," Sean said, in turn.

"Which has been partially covered."

"Ah," Sean repeated. "Would you like to come into my private suite for a drink before you go—I named it the Christopher Isherwood Suite after—"

"The man behind the *Cabaret* business, right. Originally called *Goodbye to Berlin*, I believe—a carefully worded autobiographical novel signaling him losing his virginity to another man in decadent Berlin in the interwar period."

"Yes, that one. The suite is two floors down from here. At the back of the building."

"Ah, yes, I would very much like to see your bedroom."

They had reached the suite.

"Well, this is the suite's sitting room," he said, ushering the doctor in. "What would you like to drink?"

Were those sounds of sex coming from Alex' room, Sean wondered. Who could that be in there at this time of day? He wondered if the doctor could hear what he heard, and how he reacted to it.

He quickly found out that the doctor could hear of it and how he was responding to it.

"I don't need a drink. I'd like to see your bedroom, please. There's a matter of the rest of my house call fee."

The scene in Sean's bedroom initially mirrored the one in Ricky's bedroom. Sean, naked, was twisted a quarter way on his side on the edge of his bed. Dr. Overby sat on a straight chair at the side of the bed. Overby was dressed except for his unzipped trousers. Sean was sucking his cock. In a variation, Sean's right leg was raised across Overby's chest and hooked on the doctor's right shoulder. The doctor's latex-covered left hand was up to the knuckles in Sean's ass, his finger stroking Sean's prostate, and Overby's right hand was slow-milking Sean's cock.

"Come for me, please. Relax and let it flow. Give me your come."

This time the doctor leaned over and took Sean's ejaculation in his throat when Sean came. And this time the doctor rose from his chair, went to the foot of the bed, pulled Sean's body down to him, hooked Sean's ankles on his shoulders, and fucked Sean to his own ejaculation.

Sean was lying there, cooling down, and going over the needs of the B&B for the rest of the day, the doctor's bill having fully been paid and Dr. Overby having seen himself out, when the door to the bedroom opened again. Standing in the door, provocatively leaning into the door frame, in full, hung erection, stood a smiling Brad Taggert.

"I have vetted as a bottom with Mr. Renard," he said. "I thought I should do so as a top too, if you're interested."

With a sigh, Sean bent and spread his legs again and held out his arms.

Interested in demonstrating his prowess, Brad began the fuck in a traditional Doggy style, with Sean on all fours and Brad on his feet, crouched over Sean's hips, and power driving him with his cock. He then moved into an Doggy Elevated position, with Sean's chest flat on the bed, his ass raised, and Brand on his knees between Sean's legs and capturing the wrists of both of Sean's arms and pulling them back while Brad mined his ass channel. This position changed into the higher-level position of the Doggy Twisted, with both men, buttocks to buttocks on their knees and elbows, and Brad fucking back into Sean's ass in reverse entry thrusting.

When both were ready to blow, Brad pulled Sean into a Pearly Gates position and fucked up into his ass while hand-jobbing his cock. Both men blew in great gobs of cum.

Lying there, still in that position, both panting hard, Sean said, "How did you know to end with a Pearly Gates?"

"I knew that was Mr. Renard's favorite finish, and I believe you are his favorite to finish with."

"Does he know you came straight over here from him?"

"No. Do we have to tell him?"

"No, not if you won't be a stranger to my bed."

"Just give me a whistle whenever you want it."

The Cape May Beach, 2:00 p.m.

Kent Dolan gave the other guy three minutes to leave the men's toilet and changing facility on the beach at the foot of Stockton Street before he sauntered out. He'd changed in the changing room but then had gone in the public john and waited for the cut black guy who had watched him change into his Speedo come in, which he did. Kent sat on the toilet in one of the stalls with the black guy standing in front of it like he was taking a piss and Kent putting his feet on top of the other guy's so it was hard to see that there were two guys in the stall. And then Kent, a slim redhead, but with good muscle definition, gave the black guy, who had a real club of a hard dick, a BJ just as the guy had signaled he wanted when they were in the changing room.

He thought they'd gotten away with it as he was leaving the facility, but there was a guy watching them—a slim guy, but with a more muscular build than Kent had, and not an ounce of fat on him. His veins didn't have any fat to run in, so they popped out on his skin. He was a good dozen years older than Kent, with dark brown hair, including a patch of hair on his chest around his nips and trailing down into the waistband of his Speedo. The pouch of the suit was filled out and bulged, so he was hung. Kent thought immediately of Texas, because, though he was in a Speedo with nothing on top, he was wearing cowboy boots and a cowboy hat. He had a beach towel slung over his shoulder, and he was slouching against a wall outside the changing room door, smoking a cigarette.

A couple of guys had come into the john while Kent was sucking the cock, but of course from where he was hidden, he hadn't seen anyone. He almost could recall seeing a pair of cowboy boots pause outside the stall door, but maybe just seeing this guy giving him the eye when he came out of the john influenced that sighting.

There was no use doing anything but pretending nothing had happened, though, so Kent went out onto the beach and down a few blocks to make sure the Texan wasn't following him before he spread his towel out on the sand and lay on it, on his back, his torso propped up on his elbow, and eyed the activity in the water off the beach. The water was said to be shallow here, not going beyond four feet deep for some distance.

Kent was just passing through. He'd been passing through places for a couple of months now. There was no threat of the money running out, but he should find someplace to settle down soon. He'd been a lifeguard in Galveston, so he gravitated to beaches and had taken some temporary lifeguard stints. He hadn't thought about doing that here in Cape May yet, though. He was just getting a feel for the place.

He assumed the Texan had been headed someplace else, but he'd assumed wrong. He passed along the beach between Kent and the surf line and then came back in a few minutes, laid his towel out not far from Kent, pulled his boots off, went down on his back, and covered his face with the cowboy hat. Kent wouldn't say the guy went fully down on his back, though; he was about three-quarters turned toward Kent and tucked the fingers of one hand down the front of his Speedo. There wasn't a lot of room from where the Speedo dipped to the root of the cock, so Kent's imagination told him the guy had the tip of his middle finger touching the cock root. At least an inch of dark brown pubic hair peeked out of the Speedo waistband to meet the trail of hair down his sternum and flat belly.

He likely wasn't really asleep, Kent thought. He seemed more on display. Kent didn't think he was here, next to Kent, by mistake. He'd seen or heard something back at the changing facility. He'd followed Kent here.

Kent gave him a close scrutiny. He was wiry, but he looked like he was experienced and would take good care of a guy. He certainly had an impressive bulge in his basket. And he was hard bodied. When Kent had a fantasy about being ridden by a cowboy, this could be the guy. He was older than Kent would naturally think of, but then the experience factor kicked in. And then there was that old weakness of Kent's. He was a definite submissive. When a sexy guy started touching him and saying what he wanted, Kent usually gave it to him. The black guy in the changing room had known how to signal even without words—and Kent had given him what he wanted.

Kent's idea of pleasure was giving the other guy what he wanted.

It's what got him in trouble in Texas—following the lead of another guy too long and too far into what wasn't good for him.

Kent lay back and started to doze. His was dreaming of this Texas guy fucking him, holding him down by his arms, demanding that he open his legs to him. And he did, just like that, by command. The Texan was hung like a bull and was deep inside him almost immediately. Kent snapped out of it, shook his head, and, without looking at the other guy in the flesh, rose from his towel, strode down to and into the water, and dove into the surf. He swam out to where the water was changing to a darker blue and then turned and swam back to the beach.

The other guy was propped up on his elbows, pointed at the beach, the cowboy hat on his head now, and openly watching Kent.

As Kent got back to his towel, the other guy spoke. "You swim real good. Competitive?"

"No. I do lifeguarding from time to time."

"Here in Cape May? You a local?"

"No. Down south. Texas. Galveston."

"You're a long way from Galveston."

"I sure am."

"My name is Tex," the guy said. Then he laughed. "But I'm from Maryland, not Texas. You must swim a lot or work out. You've got a good body."

So, was the guy hitting on him, Kent wondered. Probably yes. He lay down on the towel and made the mistake of turning on his side toward the guy calling himself Tex. Tex was turned toward him on his side too. And Kent could have sworn the towels were closer together now than before—and that there weren't any other sunbathers anywhere close. The afternoon was wearing on.

"I keep weight off by not getting a meal all the time. I've been drifting for a while." It wasn't completely true. He had plenty of money. But he did watch his weight. He liked to be trim. Men liked him to be trim.

"You got a name?" the guy asked.

"Kent, my name's Kent." He almost swallowed the words, though. Tex had pushed the front of his Speedo under his balls and had his cock out. It wasn't thick, but it was long. A good eight incher at least.

"Do you give a good blow job?" It was said like the guy was just asking for the time. He was holding his cock in his hand. He knew that Kent could see it—and he knew it was impressive. He didn't wait for Kent to answer. "You made some noise in sucking that black dude's cock in the changing station back there. I bet you do give good head. The black guy was smilin' when he came out. Was his as big as this one? Would you like to get your lips around this one, Kent?"

"I think I should go now," Kent said, looking away from the cock Tex was working up—but only briefly. He couldn't keep his eyes off it.

"Do you take cock too, Kent? Or do you just give blow jobs?"

"I should go now. It's going to be dark soon, and I don't have a place lined up to stay yet."

"I'll get you a place tonight. And you say you don't always get meals. I'll take you to dinner too. Come out into the ocean with me, Kent. Let's fuck around a bit. I'm standing up now." He did so, deftly stuffing his cock and balls back into the Speedo as he stood. "You first, Kent. Walk down to the water and out to where it comes up to your belly. I'll be behind you."

Emitting a little moan, Kent stood up, brushed sand off his Speedo, and walked down and out into the water. He didn't look around to see if Tex was following him, but of course he was. Kent was out about as far as Tex had told him to go when he heard someone dive into the water behind him. Tex grabbed Kent's ankles under water and upset him into the drink.

When Kent came up for air and was brushing long strands of red hair out of his face, he felt material touching his hand just under the surface of the water. "Here, hold these, under the surface," Tex commanded. He transferred both Speedos to Kent's hand. Both men were naked.

"Crouch down and face the beach and look like you're just sightseeing, watching the activity on the beach. And spread your legs. I'll be right behind you. They won't even see me from the beach. I'm gonna jack you and then I'm gonna fuck you."

For several minutes Tex was milking Kent's cock, having pulled it through his legs, was fondling and squeezing his balls, and was opening his ass up with his fingers. When he felt everything was ready, he pulled Kent back to where Kent's legs were hooked over Tex' thighs and Tex was palming his stomach. Tex worked his cock inside Kent's channel, grabbed hold of his waist under the surface of the water, and fucked him in a Bully position to an ejaculation. Kent had ejaculated when Tex was jacking him off with his cock pulled between his legs.

"Now, shall we go back to the beach and dry off? It's starting to get dark."

"Yes," Kent answered.

"And then you'll go to dinner with me and to my hotel room afterward." It wasn't a question. Tex had gauged Kent correctly.

"Yes."

The Greg Louganis Pool House, 1:15 p.m.

Derek Hillsman rose up out of the pool in the terrace at the side of the B&B. He'd been doing laps, trying to erase from his mind the raging fight the political candidate, Martin Beardsley, and his campaign manager, Jock Johnson had been having in the Alexander the Great Suite. It had started with differences of opinion in campaign strategy, but Beardsley had let slip the "N" word and the argument had gone downhill from there and gotten personal.

Derek had started leaving for the pool when Johnson was yelling, "A nigger is good enough for you— and it's good enough for your son, too."

"What in the fuck do you mean by that?" Beardsley had growled back.

Derek knew what Johnson meant about that. He'd grown to pretty much believe that Johnson was fucking Beardsley's son, who was nearly Derek's age, as well as the political candidate.

Derek heard them all the way to the pool, where he'd stripped down, dove in, and was swimming laps since 12:30. It was now 1:15 and time for his massage in the pool house from the B&B reception clerk, Jeff Stockdon. Beardsley had bought a full-body massage for each of them. Johnson's slot had been before Derek's and Beardsley's was after Derek's.

When he came up out of the water, Derek could hear and see the sex going on the pool beds beside the pool. The tennis player, Ted Landon, was on his belly at the foot of one of the low-lying pool beds, his legs mostly off the bed, and his toes pressed into the flagstones of the terrace. His hands were thrust back, grasping his buttocks, and pulling them open as far as he could. There was a look of grimace on his face. The hunk—God how Derek wanted to go another round with him—Raif, the B&B's handyman, was standing beside the pool bed. His right leg was extended over Landon's back, with the sole of his foot pressing into the back of Landon's neck, holding the young man immobile, while, left hand gripping Landon's thigh, the black bull fucked down into Landon's passage in a Doggy Twisted variation with a jet-black monster cock.

The incognito rock star, Sam Sterling, was lying on the pool bed next to them, his eyes on the action and his hand stroking his cock. Derek assumed that Landon was getting the works, being tag-team fucked by the other two. He felt himself go hard in the fantasy that it could be him. DuCorde and Sterling were cut, virile studs. They weren't older men like Beardsley and Johnson were. Of course Derek would prefer being fucked by the two younger men. And just the thought of Raif holding him immobile and twirling those sounding rods in his piss slit was enough to harden him up.

Beardsley, obviously having been given his massage, looking satiated and glassy eyed and, holding a towel in front of the privates of his naked body, brushed past Derek as Derek entered the pool house. Jeff Stockdon was standing by the massage table, pulling a jock strap on with one hand while he wiped oil off the surface of the table with the other.

He looked up and smiled, "Looks like you're more than ready for a full body treatment?"

"Pardon?" Derek asked.

"You're hard, and a very nice erection it is too. You've been thinking of me, I see." He laughed.

Derek blushed. He hadn't been thinking of Stockdon. The man had a good-enough body and the piercings and tattoo coverage was interesting—and a bit exciting—and Derek wondered what lay behind that jock pouch—but it had been the sighting of the sexier, more muscular, and black bull, Raif, he'd gotten hard for.

"I guess this means we do the front first, before you lose that," Stockdon said. "Hop up on the table on your back."

Stockdon gave Derek a good sports massage, while occasionally seizing and stroking the young man's oiled cock to keep it in erection. Derek couldn't complain that the other body parts weren't getting enough attention—even his mouth and throat. When Stockdon had Derek in a mixed state of mellow and keyed up, he pulled Derek up the table to where his head went over the edge. It was now that Derek realized that at some point Stockdon had lost his jock strap—and he was in erection. He worked on Derek's pecs and shoulders and down his side with deep massage, while his cock rubbed against Derek's cheeks. At some point, Derek opened his mouth to the cock, his head being at an angle that could take the cock deep into his throat, where, after face fucking him for a while in movements that corresponded with the massage of his chest and arms, Stockdon flooded Derek's mouth with his cum.

He then came around immediately to Derek's hips and started working the young man's calves, his thighs, the creases welding his thighs to his groin, his balls and his cock. When Stockdon was deep throating Derek's cock and had two fingers in Derek's ass, rubbing on the prostate, Derek came with a lurch and a sigh.

"Hold there for a few minutes before turning over," Stockdon said. "I need more oil." With just that warning, Stockdon headed for the mansion.

Mellow and sleepy, Derek rolled onto his stomach, turned his face toward the pool, and watched Raif, Sam, and Ted in a three-way fuck on one of the pool beds. The three were in a Double Dildo position. Landon was lying at the head of the pool bed, his head arched over the top of the bed, his arms stretched out in a cruciform position, and his legs spread and bent over Sterling's thighs. Sterling was lying with his head toward the foot of the pool bed. His cock was buried in Landon's ass. DuCorde was kneel with one knee on the pool bed at Sterling's head, where Sterling was handling and servicing DuCorde's cock with his mouth. DuCorde was slowly jacking Landon's cock off.

Stockdon was back with a bottle of oil. "Here we go again, baby," he said as he started pouring oil up and down Derek's back and legs and, especially into his buttocks crack. He worked, quickly and expertly up and down Derek's back, paying a lot of attention to Derek's shoulders and shoulder blades and the meat of his thighs and calves. He lifted both arms and massaged down them and into the arm pits. Then he went to the small of the back and down to the buttocks, kneading and rolling and separating them. His oiled fingers rubbed over the hole and he bent and blew into it. Derek quietly mewed and the hole puckered for Stockdon.

Stockdon was fingering the hole and stroking the prostrate, giving Derek a second ejaculation. An oiled dildo was produced from somewhere, Stockdon instructed him to raise his buttocks a bit, and Derek moaned as Stockdon worked his ass. Stockdon told Derek to raise his pelvis up more, and then Stockdon was up on the table, covering Derek's body himself, fucking his ass, and reaching under Derek's belly to stroke his cock to a third ejaculation.

Lost to the massage and fuck, Derek was groaning and whispering "Yes, yes, fuck me, fuck me, just like that," as he looked over toward the pool to see Landon on his belly on a pool bed, with Sterling stretched out on him, his cock fucking Landon, and DuCorde stretched out on Sterling's back fucking him in an Anal Train, when . . .

All hell broke out. Sean Temple was running out of the mansion and yelling something about an accident, with a man trailing behind him in beltless trousers and valiantly trying to keep the trousers from slipping down his legs as he ran.

The Christopher Isherwood Suite, 2:00 p.m.

Detective-Lieutenant David Pollack was on his back, naked, on Sean's bed, receiving his periodic protection payment, as Sean sat on his midsection, his hands palming Pollack's pecs, and giving Pollack's cock a Cowboy ride. The detective's shoot off was cut off, Sean having already ejaculated up the detective's belly, by the loud knock at the door.

"Sean? Sean? You in there?" Alex was bellowing. "You need to come downstairs. And you need to bring that cop with you."

Descending the stairs to the first floor, both of them only in their trousers, Sean and Pollack came upon the body of Jock Johnson at the foot of the stairs in the entrance foyer. It was clear that his neck was broken. It was equally clear that he was dead. The body must have bounced off the banister on the way down the stairs, as a section of the banister was broken away from the stairs and hanging down into the passage back to the music room and the library.

"I'm going back upstairs to dress and call in forensics," Detective Pollack said, generally making his way past the body and up the stairs again. "Gather everyone here in the sunroom off the dining room," he said to Sean.

"Surely it's an accident—and the privacy of the guests," Sean said. "You know maintaining their privacy is important, David."

"I have to talk to them to determine what's what. And I won't keep written notes. If you can think of a way to keep them anonymous—"

"Can we identify the guests by the name of the room they're in—at least until you can rule out anything but an accident? We, of course, want to keep their identities out of the newspaper. It's OK to use the names of those on staff here."

"We can try that, yes. You realize I'll have to do some two stepping to keep this quiet and out of the press." The look he gave Sean before he turned and headed upstairs, still holding his trousers up with one hand on the waistband, spoke volumes of how much in the way of services for protection would have to be ratcheted up.

As soon as Pollack disappeared up the stairs, Sean turned to Alex. "Have you noticed anything wrong with the treads at the top of the stairs?"

"No, it's all newly laid. I'm sure he tripped on his own feet," Alex answered. "This will just be a tragic accident."

"I sure hope so," Sean responded. "Can you roust everyone out and get them to the sunroom? I'll get to Jeff." When he did track down Jeff, who was still in the pool house wiping oil off his hands and other body parts, Sean sent Jeff on a separate errand.

"Quick as you can, switch the registration books and bring the backup one to the sunroom. Erase the name in the Brian Boitano Suite for the weekend and put Jock Johnson's true name in there." The purpose of keeping two sets of registration books was that the second set, written in an erasable pen, included names of men paid off to say they were in those rooms those nights, as needed.

The Michelangelo Sun Porch, 2:15 p.m.

"Anybody missing?" Detective Pollack asked when it had appeared everyone—guests and staff—had arrived and settled around the tables.

Finishing looking around, Sean said. "The Rock Hudson Suite checked out at 10:00. The Renée Richards Suite isn't here. Neither is the Alexander the Great Suite Number One."

"Number One?" Pollack asked. Sean was referring to Martin Beardsley, who hadn't been found in the building or at the pool.

"Yes, there are two bedrooms in that suite. Number Two," he said, gesturing to Derek Hillsman, "is in the other bedroom. The two of them are colleagues, as was the Brian Boitano Suite, which is the deceased."

"Any way to try to contact this Number One?" Pollack asked.

"I can try calling him on his cell phone," Derek volunteered.

"Yes, do that," Pollack answered, and Derek withdrew to the dining room.

"And about this Renée Richards," Pollack said. At that moment Mel Duncan arrived, small suitcase in hand and the remnants of makeup on his face. He looked somewhat bewildered.

"I couldn't get in the front door," he said, "I had to come through the parking lot and heard you all in here. And there was a police car pulling up to the front of the inn."

"Ah, that will be the forensics team," Pollack said, standing. "Where have you just been?" he asked Duncan as he moved to the door.

"I was at a bar," Duncan answered.

"I saw him at a bar earlier today and I work there part time," Brad Taggert piped up. "I could call the bar and verify that he was there for the time you are interested in."

At the door to the dining room, Pollack said, "Yes, do that."

Still looking bewildered, Duncan was ushered to a seat beside Alex, who whispered what was going on to him. Taggert went into the dining room to make his call, reporting to Pollack, when he came back through the dining room after letting the forensics team in, that Duncan's time was accounted for. By then Hillsman had gotten hold of Beardsley on his cell phone too.

"The other man in the Alexander the Great Suite is up in Toms River at a political event. I talked to someone who is with him there, who verified he was there, although his appearance was a surprise. His campaign had said he had another engagement then. I saw him last when I was going for a massage a little after 1:00. He had just gotten his." After saying this, Hillsman was a little perplexed. Now that he thought of it, Beardsley's massage was supposed to be after his. Jock Johnson was supposed to get his massage first. If Jock Johnson had made his appointment, he wouldn't be falling down a staircase and breaking his neck at the same time as he was being massaged.

"He's off the hook, then," Pollack said, with a bit of relief. He knew damn well who Alexander the Great Suite Number One was. "The cook said he found the body at 2:00 but that he'd used those stairs fifteen minutes earlier and there was no body. So, with that fifteen-minute timeframe, Number One couldn't have pushed the deceased down the stairs and now be in Toms River."

Back on the sun porch, Pollack asked if any of the other guests or staff were missing. "The Don Lemon Room isn't here, which is strange. He has kept to his room since he arrived on Saturday. And beyond that, the only other guest missing is someone who checked into the Harvey Milk Room just this morning, but he left soon thereafter and hasn't come back yet. And, oh, one of the staff members, Ricky Sanchez, is still upstairs, on the fourth floor, in his room. He was injured earlier in the day and isn't really able to be moving around, let alone pushing guests down the stairs."

"And so, now," Pollack asked those assembled, "where was everyone who is here between 1:45 and 2:00, and whose time is not yet accounted for?"

"You know where I was," Sean said.

Jeff Stockdon spoke up. "I can speak for several others. Mr.—"

"Room identifiers for the guests, please, Jeff."

"Oh, OK. The Alexander the Great Suite Number Two here was on my massage table in the pool house—and I was there too, of course. And three others, the Freddy Mercury Suite, the Cole Porter Suite, and the handyman, Raif DuCorde, were at the pool, where I had a line of sight on them the whole time."

"Val here and I were in the kitchen, starting on dinner preparations," Alex said. "We're open to the public tonight."

"But you found the body and were back and forth on that staircase, so you—"

". . . don't have an alibi for not being there when the man went down the stairs," Alex filled in. The two men gave each other hard looks for a few seconds. Pollack looked away first.

"So, that's everyone then," Pollack said, with relief evident in his voice. "It looks like it can be written up as an accident—I hope. Now, I want all of the guests to go back to their rooms and hold tight there, doors locked, for a couple of hours. Is there a back staircase to this building?"

"Yes, reached through the kitchen, which can be accessed through the dining room," Sean answered.

"But, why—?" Mel Duncan started to ask, still bewildered enough to be slow in the uptake.

"The place is going to be swarming with police for a while," Pollack said. "I don't think any of you guests want to run into any of them and have to answer questions. Most of the activity is going to be gathered around the front staircase."

"Oh," Duncan said.

"But what about those of us who work here?" Val said.

"You're members of the community and you have a reason to be here in what this inn is—you work here. You aren't guests choosing to come to a place like this with the hope of privacy."

"Oh," Val answered.

"Now, on your way, everyone. I will keep this as buttoned down as I can."

Sean broke in at this point. "We're sure this was just a bad accident," he said to the assembled guests. "Please don't let it upset your stay or any plans you have."

As the guests started moving into the dining room to access the rear staircase in the kitchen, Pollack turned to Sean and said, "If this works, I'm going to own your ass big time."

"I realize that," Sean answered. He didn't really care all that much beyond hoping that Pollack could keep the lid on the death. Pollack was very good in bed, if a bit forceful.

Siesta Time all Over the Inn, 4:00 p.m.

Nap time at the GayLords B&B, though no one was napping, except for Ricky Sanchez, who was recovering from his wounds in the Chris Steele Room.

Cory Townsend had returned from his buying mission at a sleazy strip mall just north of the town limits and had sneaked his bag of goodies up to the Don Lemon Room just before making his appointment for a massage in the pool house from Jeff Stockdon.

Stockdon supposedly was working on his spine alignment at 4:00 p.m., in a position invention of his own that he called a Rocking Horse, a position not in Alex' gay Kama Sutra bag of tricks. Townsend was belly down on the massage table, with only his belly touching the table. His ankles were on Stockdon's shoulders and Stockdon had him in a full Nelson, with Stockdon's arms under Townsend's arm pits and Stockdon's fists locked behind Townsend's neck. Townsend's body was bowed back at both ends, Stockdon's cock was deep inside Townsend's ass, and Townsend was squeaking and huff and puffing as Stockdon rocked his body back and forth, providing the pumping motion of his cock.

At 4:00 Brad Taggert was helping Derek Hillsman from being consumed by concern that one of his colleagues was dead and the other one had deserted him here in Cape May, by orchestrating a flip-flop Cowboy fuck with him in what had been Martin Beardsley's bed in the Alexander the Great Suite.

At that moment Ted Landon was sitting on Sam Sterling's cock on the piano bench in the Leonard Bernstein Music Room, with his head turned to suck on Raif DuCorde's cock. Raif had found the two musicians working on a song in the music room and had easily convinced them to take a break.

At 3:30 new guests had begun to arrive and Val was busy restocking and cleaning up the Rock Hudson and Elton John Suites. The three first arrivals didn't care that they had to wait for their rooms. The porn stars Jack Doff and Deep Diver were fucking on a sofa in the Truman Capote Library behind the music room. Deep Diver was diving deep in Jack Doff in a Folded Deck Chair position, Jack Doff wedged into the sofa with his legs jack-knifed into his body and his arms encasing his calves, while, his forehead plastered to Doff's, Deep Diver leveraged off his feet on the floor and fucked Doff's ass. Denny Walker, a cameraman, roamed around with his video camera picking up various interesting aspects of the deep fuck.

At 4:00 Sean rolled off Alex after a completed Pearly Gates fuck, and the two lay there, in each other's arms, panting and thinking of the chores for the rest of the day.

"I have to get back to the kitchen soon to complete tonight's service."

"Many reservations?"

"Not many, but it's our first night and we didn't heavily advertise the open dinner service. We have the movie crew coming in. That will take a couple of the tables."

"Do you think it was too soon to open the rooms up for porn movies."

"No. It's good income. Are you going to let them film you?"

Sean laughed. "If they ask, offer good money, and let me wear a mask. You know they've already signed Raif."

"I'm not a bit surprised."

"How about the new guy, Brad?" asked Sean.

"Oh, I wouldn't be surprised if they sign him too."

"No, I mean do you think he'll work out?"

"Didn't he work you out?" Alex asked, showing Sean a "you can't fool me" smile.

"Yes, as a matter of fact he did."

"Then I think he'll work out here just fine," Alex answered. "What about you? What do you have before dinner."

"Pollack's coming back for another interrogation at 5:30."

"Who is he interrogating?" Alex asked.

"Just me. Someone has to pay for the extra protection services."

"Do you mind?"

"Not really."

"Tell me this is working out."

"It's a bit rough at the start," Sean answered. "But we knew it would be. We didn't know anyone would tumble down our stairs and break his neck, of course. We didn't factor in an accident like this."

"If it was an accident."

"You don't think it was an accident?" Sean asked, propping himself up on an elbow to look down into Alex' face. His other hand was busy with Alex' cock.

"Just a feeling I have."

"Well, don't let any of the guests know you think it might have been anything but an accident. And what are we to do about your feelings?" Sean asked.

"Well, for what I'm feeling at the moment, I'd like you to give me your very best Cowboy ride."

Sean did just that, barely having time to shower before Detective Pollack arrived to interrogate Sean in a Bodyguard Elevated position, with Sean kneeling on a deep window sill in his bedroom at 5:30, while Alex and Val were busy in the kitchen preparing for the dinner service. Pollack stood behind Sean, one hand palming Sean's belly and the other cupping his chin, pulling his head back into the hollow of Pollack's shoulder, as Pollack took his extra police protection fee by pumping Sean's ass to an ejaculation.

The Gore Vidal Dining Room, 7:30 p.m.

The dining room that evening certainly wasn't packed with guests, but the eight men at two tables helped to keep it from looking deserted. These were actors and film crew members who had rented bedrooms and periodic access to the public rooms in the B&B through Tuesday night to film a series of gay male pornographic movies. There were four actors with the crew—plus Raif had already been signed to perform, and they were talking with Brad—two camera men, a director, and a "Mr. Fixit" for any and all problems that might arise. They all had healthy appetites and went for the "meat and potatoes" items on Alex' menu.

Throughout the meal, the director flirted with Val as she served them and one of the porn actors felt up Brad, the other waiter, as well. Val and Brad flirted back, as they were encouraged to do by inn policy.

There were three men and women couples who came to dine from the outside as well as two man-and-man couples who were locals. All of these were at tables for two. All appeared to be satisfied with their meal and the service, and a couple of the male diners complimented Sean, acting as the maitre d' hotel, when they left and said they'd be back. One of the men even asked, with interest, if the eight men eating together were locals and was a bit disappointed when Sean said they weren't, without volunteering that they were staying at the inn.

"Funny," one local said. "I thought I'd seen one or two of them before."

I bet you have, Sean thought—in porn movies. What he said was, "I think they're all from the West Coast."

Mel Duncan was eating alone and was looking rather morose and withdrawn at the beginning of the service, but Brad Taggert paid him more than his share of attention during the service, leaning his head down and whispering to him as he danced by, and Duncan left the dining room with a broad smile on his face and an almost girlish spring in his step

Cory Townsend, the virtual recluse up to that point, came down to take dinner and sat with Derek Hillsman. The two were in a deep conversation, which surprised Sean, and he might be even more surprised to have known that Townsend was querying Hillsman on what he might know, sexually, about the handyman, Raif DuCorde. Townsend appeared both fascinated and horrified by Hillsman's description of the technique of sounding.

"And there's such a set of wands—you called them rods—in the inn now?" Townsend asked.

"I'm sure they're floating around somewhere," Hillsman answered. Alex was visiting the tables as the service concluded and was beaming at the compliments he received on the food and the presentation. There had been just enough patrons for his opening night—he was easily able to keep up with the orders and have them out quickly and piping hot. After speaking briefly to Townsend and Hillsman at their table, he put his mouth to Hillsman's ear and whispered something. Hillsman smiled and nodded his head.

Raif, Sam Sterling, and Ted Landon weren't there for dinner. They had decided to check out the local eateries and bars. For dinner they wound up at the Pilot House Restaurant in the Carpenter's Square area a couple of blocks inland from the inn on Decatur. Sterling and Landon wanted to find someplace afterward that had a rock band, but this being Sunday and basically a traditionally family beach resort, they gave up and were headed back to the inn by 9:30.

Raif would have had to split from them about then anywhere, as he had a service call to go to at 10:00.

There was one other couple there for dinner, and one of them was a guest at the inn. The man calling himself Tex, the tall, wiry man in the cowboy clothes, appeared for dinner with another, younger blond and a bit uncertain, man with him. He had brought his "in the ocean conquest" from the beach, Kent Dolan, with him to the dining room. There wasn't a doubt in Sean's mind in seeing the two of them and how Tex took and maintained control that Tex had brought the young man back to the inn to nail him. That was permitted in the inn's loose room use policy, though, so Sean didn't pay too much attention to them.

There was always the danger that a guest would book for the night, bring another man—probably a rentboy—in to fuck, and then abscond that night and somehow avoid paying the bill. Tex had prepaid for a night, though, so that wasn't a problem in this case.

Sean could see in their remote, shadowed corner of the dining room that Tex was putting the moves on the young man. He kept insinuating his knees between the other man's thighs and, by dessert, Tex had a bare foot pressed into the young man's crotch, and the young man was massaging it.

Yep, Sean thought, those two are going straight from here to the bed in the Harvey Milk Room.

Harvey Milk Room, 8:30 p.m.

Sean was not quite right about Tex and Kent going at each other on the bed in Tex' room straight from dinner. They didn't make the bed. They were only half way between the door to the room and the bed, and Tex was totally dominating Kent, taking him in a Fire Hydrant position, with Kent leaning over the back of a club chair, his elbow on the far arm of the chair, his torso twisted so he could watch Tex fuck him, and standing behind his buttocks, Kent's left leg raised and supported by Tex' left hand, as Tex fucked him in a side split. All of Tex' clothes except for his cowboy hat, boots, leather wrist bands, and a red bandana around his neck were strewn between the door and the chair. All of Kent's clothes other than his unbuttoned shirt were in similar disarray on the floor.

The Ladies Room in the Back Hall, First Floor, 8:45 p.m.

The film crew had rented the basement rooms for the evening and they had just taken a break from filming a sex scene between Jack Doff and Deep Diver back in the corner of the Jack Kerouac Billiards Room, where a couple of pieces of exercise equipment and mats were kept. The director, Hal Burton, late forties, graying pony tail and thickish around the middle—a porn star himself in the early nineties—had gone out on the inn's front porch during the break to catch a cigarette. Coming back in, he encountered Val, in her white blouse, black skirt, medium-height black pumps, and coquettish smile, coming out of the kitchen after completing the kitchen cleanup.

The two looked at each other a couple of seconds and with a bit more interest than would be normal for two strangers passing in the hall. Burton pulled Val into the ladies room—there being no danger anyone would see them there, as Val cleaned the room and it would only be used during the dinner service—and pressed her body up against the wall. As they kissed, Val whispered a "Yes," lifted her legs, one after the other, to aid Burton in slipping her panties off, and then turned a cheek to the wall, clutched at the back of Burton's head and panted heavily as Burton jacked her cock.

Val having spouted quickly, Burton turned her and pushed her to her knees, pulled his cock out of the gym shorts he'd been wearing, and face fucked her.

Val, still a neophyte, but in awe of a movie director—any kind of movie director—let Burton manipulate her like she was a rag doll.

Burton fucked her up against the wall in a Suspended Congress position, pushing Val's back up and down the wall with the strength of his cock, with Val's legs wrapped around the small of Burton's back, her skirt bunched up around her waist, and her arms flung around Burton's neck.

The Harvey Milk Room, 8:45 p.m.

Tex fucked Kent in a Soaring Eagle, with Kent on his back at the base of the bed, the small of his back running up the foot of the bed, his legs spread, and beating his own cock with his right hand, as legs on the bed and torso suspended over Kent's body, Tex buried his fists in the carpet to the right of Kent's head and fucked down into him in a side split.

The Don Lemon Room, 9:00 p.m.

Cory Townsend was nervously roaming around his room, waiting for 10:00. He laid out the purchases he'd made at the adult store earlier in the afternoon: the restraints, the string of beads, and the dildo. He picked up the black leather box that Derek Hillsman had retrieved for him from somewhere and was letting him borrow for the night. He opened the box and ran his fingers over the cool metal rods. He shuddered and licked his lips, but it wasn't because he was cold.

Alexander the Great Suite, 9:00 p.m.

Derek Hillsman was trying out Alex, euphoric from his first, successful, he thought, dinner service in the inn, on the bed that Martin Beardsley had vacated earlier in the day. Or, rather, Alex was slowly introducing Derek to exotic and demanding male Kama Sutra positions the young media consultant had never known existed before.

Alex started with a Deep Impact, standing on the floor at the foot of the bed, his cock thrust inside Derek, on the small of his back and his legs raised and spread with him grasping his own ankles and Alex coordinating the thrust of his cock in Derek's passage with the stroking of the young man's cock. As the fuck became more intense, Alex came up on the bed, shoved his knees under Derek's buttocks while Derek hooked his ankles behind Alex' waist, and Alex continued to pump him in a Butterfly position. Moving to the exotic, Alex brought them to the first ejaculation in the Bumper Cars position, with Derek cantilevering off the bed with his cheek on the floor and his hands gripping Alex' ankles, while, reversed on him, Alex grabbed Derek's ankles and pounded his ass in a reverse fucking.

Derek slid to the floor at the foot of the bed at the finish of that, panting hard, as Alex said, "I'm going to take a break—gotta piss and cover for a second go at you."

A second go, Derek thought, with a moan. But he watched Alex' firm buttocks roll as the man went off to the bathroom. While he waited and cooled down a bit, the thought of the break taken got lodged in his mind and connected with something else that had happened yesterday, something connected with the death of Jock Johnson.

But then Alex was back, in full erection, and was pulling Derek back up on the bed and on top of him, Alex' back on the bed and Derek's back above Alex' chest, as, for twenty minutes more, without ever taking his cock out of Derek's channel, he maneuvered the young man from a Fusion fuck, where the two faced each other, their thigh's crossed, both of them raising their buttocks with hands propping them up behind there reclined torsos, and Alex mining Derek's depths. At Alex' direction, Derek turned his body around to the Crab position, with Derek raised on both his hands and his feet several inches off Alex' body, while Alex held his waist and fucked up into his channel, to the more intimate Cowboy Reverse Asian, with Derek's hands buried in the hollow where Alex' arms met his shoulders and both men with spread and bent legs, and Alex reaching around to jack Derek's cock. The conclusion came in Alex' favorite Pearly Gates position, holding Derek tight against his chest, Derek's head next to Alex', the two kissing, while Alex squeezed Derek's cock, causing it to spout toward the ceiling, while Alex filled out the bulb of his condom deep in Derek's channel.

"You know, I wonder about Jock Johnson's death," Derek said hesitatingly.

"I'm sure it was just a tragic accident," Alex responded. "You know what I wonder?"

109

"What?"

"Whether we have the time and inclination for me to get a new rubber."

They were inclined and made time.

Later, exhausted, Derek lay, unable to go to sleep, as timelines and circumstances of the previous day's events worried his mind.

Harvey Milk Room, 9:10 p.m.

Tex had Kent immobilized in the center of the room in a Bully position, Kent's body draped on Tex' torso, Tex' legs bent enough that Kent's feet were set on Tex' knees. Kent's ass was mounted on Tex' cock again.

"Yes, yes, I'll like that," Kent was murmuring as Tex clicked a pair of handcuffs on Kent's wrists.

"Don't be too sure of that, little darlin'," Tex muttered.

Front Foyer, 9:30 p.m.

Tex hustled Kent past Raif as he was coming up the front steps to return to the inn to prepare for his 10:00 p.m. appointment.

Both Tex and Kent were dressed, but Kent was handcuffed and being manhandled by Tex.

"Hey, what gives?" Raif asked, having been nearly knocked off balance.

"We're checking out," Tex said. "I left the room key on the reception desk counter. The room's paid up. When you see one of the owners tell them I got what I came for and left."

"What are you doing with this guy?" Raif asked, pointing to Kent, who looked like a frightened rabbit. Raif's first impression was that the Texan was taking the kid for a last ride.

"I'm a bounty hunter operating out of Fort Worth," Tex said, producing documents that he put under Raif's nose. "This here's my bounty. I've run after him all up the Eastern Coast. He's wanted in Fort Worth for bail jumping on a stolen car charge. Just give my regards to the owners. Nice little inn they've got here. I might be back when I'm not on the job. Might even be interested in going a round or two with you."

And then Tex was hustling Kent toward a Ford truck parked out on the street.

"Well, have a good trip," Raif said in their wake.

Tex turned and laughed, shaking Kent by the scruff of his neck. "Bounties not big on this one, but I figure if I fuck him all the way back to Texas I'll have earned a good fee—and will have knocked all the fight out of him."

The Jack Kerouac Billiards Room, 9:45 p.m.

The four porn actors were gathered around a billiards table lit up with arc lights, each holding one of Val's wrists or ankles in a spread-eagle position. Brad Taggert, his knees pushed under her buttocks, with her black skirt bunched up around her belly button, was taking first honors in Missionary fucking her on the billiards table, while the two cameramen waltzed around taking in the tableau from various angles. The porn actors would all get their turn during the filming, with Hal Burton directing everything with hand signals from behind the cameras.

To make clear that Val was a transvestite, her blouse was left closed over her jutting falsies, and her dick was clearly in evidence in all shots. For effect her panties were hooked on one of her ankles.

It was Brad's first turn under his new contract with the movie company. Val got on the table willingly too, although the next hour would show just how challenged she was by this. The director's cash offer and promise that he'd take her to bed with him that night if she debuted in the movie—plus being star struck that someone would put her in a movie—were enough to make her willing—in theory and for now. Her willingness didn't lower the movie value of how new and taxing this all was for her.

The Greg Louganis Pool House, 9:45 p.m.

As his massage appointment was approaching from the house, Jeff Stockdon interrupted the counting of the stack of bills that had been slipped to him earlier in the afternoon and tucked them away in his athletic bag along with the wallet and wristwatch he'd lifted from a room.

In the candlelight from the tea candles strewn around the pool room, the two men stood facing each other. Stockdon and the movie company's Mr. Fixit, Hanyu Li, untied the sashes of their robes at the same time, let them fall open to reveal all, and eyed each other through slitted eyes for several seconds. Neither seemed disappointed.

"Get up on the massage table on your back," Stockdon said. "I see something that needs relief right away." He hadn't known what to expect. He'd never done a Chinese man before. He found that Li was much like any other man—and so aroused by the thought of receiving a full-body massage that he already was hard.

Twenty minutes later Stockdon had already given a fully cooperative Li an oiled hand job and prostate rub to ejaculation and Li, his head suspended over the end of the table while Stockdon worked his torso muscles, had already sucked Stockdon to an erection, when Stockdon came up on the table. Saying, "This will stretch your leg muscles and help with flexibility," he pressed Li's bent legs hard into his chest, rolling up the man's pelvis at the same time, and thrust his cock deep inside Li's channel in a Deep Impact fuck, starting to work on an entirely different form of stretching.

As Li howled to the rafters of the pool house, and cried out a litany of, "Fuck it, fuck it. God, yes, fuck it!" Stockdon set his mind to what he'd buy first with the money in his bag and who best to sell the credit cards to that were in the wallet.

The Freddy Mercury Suite, 10:00 p.m.

Sam Sterling, the rock star, and Ted Landon, the pro tennis player and music composer wannabe, arrived back at the inn more sober than they had planned to be before finding out that Cape May rolled up the sidewalks on a Sunday night. They looked drunk, though; they were embracing each other, not walking a straight line, and were throwing snatches of musical runs and lyrics at each other in an attempt to build a song.

When they reached the room, Sam lit up a toke, took up his guitar, and they just continued working together on the song. They didn't even mention sex. They were all fucked out for the moment and both realized that they both would leave the next day and that they hadn't composed a song together yet.

It suddenly was important to them both that they do that.

Along about midnight, they both keeled over on the bed, in an embrace—but both snoring rather than fucking.

The Don Lemon Room, 10:00 p.m.

Raif used his master key to quietly open the door to the room. It was dark when he slid into the room, but

113

Cory Townsend flipped on the nightstand light as soon as he knew Raif was in the room and had had time to slip off his clothes and leave them, folded, near the door.

Raif took on the expression of a deer in the headlights when the light was switched on, but then he laughed.

Cory was lying on his back on the bed, naked and his back propped up on pillows against the headboard. He was holding restraints with leads in one hand and a dildo and string of beads in the other. "Can you bind me and do me with these tonight?" he asked. "And afterward will you show me what sounding feels like." He turned his eyes to the nightstand and the black leather case sitting on it that he'd gotten from Derek Hillsman.

Raif laughed and moved toward the bed.

The Christopher Isherwood Suite, 10:45 p.m.

After leaving Derek Hillsman exhausted but satiated in the Alexander the Great Suite, Alex had gone to check on the preparations for the breakfast service in the kitchen. They weren't as far along as he expected them to be. Val hadn't done what he asked her to do and she wasn't in the kitchen. He quickly put everything to rights and then climbed the stairs to the Christopher Isherwood Suite.

He was weary and fucking Hillsman had taken a lot out of him. He didn't feel like having sex, but he didn't feel like sleeping alone tonight either. Sean had recently said the Alex was all Kama Sutra fuck, and no romance. But Alex was feeling romantic tonight, and he realized that it was Sean who affected him that way. Just cuddling and sleeping within each other's embrace tonight was all Alex wanted to do. Entering the suite he padded over to the door to Sean's bedroom.

Some instinct told him not to knock. It probably was no more, however, than hearing the heavy breathing of two, not one, people in the bedroom. He cracked the door. They were asleep, but there was every reason to believe that they'd had sex before going to sleep and that his brother, Eddie's, cock was most likely sheathed in Sean ass passage. Sean was on his back, his legs open, and Eddie was lying between them. One of Sean's arms was trailing off to the side and the other was embracing Eddie's back. Eddie's arms were raised above Sean's head and his head was laying next to Sean's, his lips turned to Sean's cheek.

The two looked maddeningly peaceful and satisfied in their pose.

Alex' attention went to the floor beside the bed. The two spent condoms didn't make him frown, but the tit clamps connected with a chain and the string of anal balls gave him pause. His appetites were entirely different from Eddie's. Alex had to wonder which Sean preferred.

With a sad sigh and feeling of defeat and concern that he couldn't rationalize, Alex turned and went to his own bed—uncharacteristically alone. Exhausted, he drifted off to sleep almost immediately.

The Don Lemon Room, 11:00 p.m.

Cory Townsend was on his back, spread-eagled and tied off with restraints at the four corners of the bed. He was gagged—willingly—with a ball gag, having been told that he'd probably otherwise be screaming the house down with what Raif was going to do to him. He was trembling, sweating profusely. His eyes were big as saucers and he'd bitten nearly through the rubber of the ball gag.

Looks were deceiving, though. He was getting exactly what he'd asked for from exactly the man he wanted to get it from—the stranger who had already

115

visited and fucked him, bound and gagged, a couple of times.

Raif had his knees running up under Cory's buttocks, which were raised to receive Raif's deeply buried cock. Raif was holding Cory's hard cock steady with one hand as he slowly twirled the fourth sounding rod Cory's urethra cannel had received that night.

The Brian Boitano Suite, 11:30 p.m.

Forgetting all about the preparations she had been supposed to have made for the next day's breakfast, Val was on her knees and elbows on the bed, with the movie director Hal Burton crouched over her from behind and giving her a Doggy fuck, the slide of the cock extra loose because of how wide Val had been reamed by the gang bang movie earlier in the evening. The director had a hand under Val's belly and was stroking her cock.

There was no indication in how Val was taking the plowing that she had been a virgin just the day before.

The René Richards Suite, Midnight

Mel Duncan, tricked out in a Teddy, a wig, the black mesh stockings, and the red spike heels, was lying on his back on his bed, his arms flung out wide, in cruciform supplication, his legs spread, and his torso arching back to the bed, with a strong arm under the small of his back. Brad Taggert was crouching between his legs, his mouth sucking on one of Duncan's exposed, rouged nipples, while he fucked Duncan deep.

Duncan was mewing, purring, and sighing his appreciation.

Across the Mansion, 2:00 a.m.

All was quiet across GayLords Inn, Jeff Stockdon having just departed after ferreting out his athletic bag from under a counter in the pool house to take back to his own rooms on the other side of Cape May. No way he was going to let this and its contents out of his sight.

Chapter Four: Day Three, Monday

Renée Richards Suite, 6:00 a.m.

Mel Duncan was standing in front of the dresser, adjusting the knot of his neck tie in the mirror. He was having trouble focusing on the tie, because he could see to the bed in the reflection of the mirror, where the beautiful, blond, muscular, almost thuggish Brad Taggert was stretched out. Brad was propped up on an elbow and fondling his balls absentmindedly with the other hand.

Duncan could see that Brad was watching him dress in his male clothes and had a smile on his face that Mel took, gratefully, as genuine as Brad couldn't see that the lawyer was watching him.

Brad was a godsend to Mel. The lawyer only now realized that he had arranged this weekend with his close friend and law partner, Jack Wilder, because he was afraid that their relationship was deteriorating. Jack himself probably didn't realize it, Mel thought, but he was trying too hard to please Mel. Mel wasn't sure that Jack was completely pleased with the arrangement anymore, but there was no way to gracefully withdraw from it even if he realized that.

Since Jack had left the previous day, Mel had had time to think about their relationship. They were close, possibly too close. And Mel was never really comfortable with Jack being OK with Mel wanting to fuck in drag. Mel was still in a power position over Jack in the office. Maybe it was time to give his colleague breathing room and to think of Jack more as a friend than as a lover. Maybe Jack would be happier with that too.

Duncan didn't need the sex in drag all that often. And here, Brad Taggert, young, vigorous, and a real stud, hadn't batted an eyelash over Mel's preferences—not the other day in Phillip's Bar or here. And he gave a total fuck. Not that Mel required anything special in a fuck. He preferred a romantic Missionary position, and Brad accommodated him without any sign of disparagement. Mel thought that maybe six or seven sessions a year with a willing stud like Brad would be enough for him—and that then Jack could just be his closest friend.

The tie taken care of, he turned around and spread his arms. He was in tailored slacks, a stark-white shirt, with a red tie and a vest that matched the slacks. "There, how do I look? The lawyer's power suit. Better then I look in the black stockings and red heels?"

"You look good in anything—and out of everything," Brad said. "Come closer to the bed and I'll show you how good you look to me." Brad had worked his cock up into a half erection.

"You know just what to say to me, but, alas, we don't have time for that. You will be needed downstairs for the breakfast service shortly, and I have some paperwork to do to justify this 'business' trip I've been on."

Mel was clearly pleased by what Brad had said, even knowing that his body couldn't look that good to a twenty-two-year-old stud. But Brad was good at what he did—very, very good.

"Brad . . . might you possibly give me a phone number and see me—do what you do with me—several

119

times a year?" He hesitated to broach the subject. What if Brad laughed at him; what if he said, "No way."

"I would enjoy that," Brad said. "Of course I do this for a living. If I came to you, it would be $100 plus travel and upkeep expenses. I could do you three or four times for the hundred bucks, so it wouldn't come out to be too expensive. If I'm working here and you are checked in here, it comes with the cost of the room."

"Ah, I didn't know it came with the room," Mel said. "I've left something for you on the dresser. I won't take it back, though, of course . . . especially if you're willing to . . . service . . . me again."

"I'm sorry if mentioning money seems crass, but . . ."

"No, not at all. I like a man who is honest and straightforward."

"I was going to say . . . but that I wouldn't say I was available at all outside of my contract with the inn if I wasn't happy to be with you. I enjoy fucking you."

Duncan didn't, in the least, resent Brad's connection of the sex with the money Mel would have to pay. In his business, he did, in fact, admire a man of candor who was straightforward in his dealings. Mel was old enough that he didn't mind paying for it from a young stud. He was dumb enough not to know that, to some extent, he was paying his law partner for it as well in the form of favoritism.

Don Lemon Room, 6:30 a.m.

Cory Townsend woke up with a start—possibly from the sound of the door to the corridor closing. He was spread-eagled on his bed, legs bent and spread. He no longer was in restraints. The ones he'd bought were neatly coiled and laying on the night stand. His ass was sore and so was his cock. Raif was gone, but Cory still felt like he was filled and stretched. Reaching down, he pulled the dildo out of his ass. And in brushing past his cock, he saw the head of a rod peeking out of his piss slit. He held his breath and moaned as he pulled the road out of his penis and felt the burble of cum that had been brought to the surface with the extraction.

He stretched, arched his back, and sighed deeply. He never before felt so alive, so in touch with his senses—so free and satisfied. So fucked. Oh, well, he had to be back in Baltimore by 5:00 p.m. to go on TV at 6:00. He rolled over, with a groan of highly satisfying aches and pain, and padded toward the shower, whistling a happy tune.

Freddy Mercury Suite, 6:05 a.m.

Raif quietly opened the door to the suite. He was returning the borrowed box of sounding rods, but he also thought he had time for another threesome with Sam Sterling and Ted Landon before he had to report to the swimming pool at 11:00. The movie crew had rented the pool for an orgy movie filming, and Raif had been hired to be part of the orgy.

He found Sam spooning Ted's body into his and both quietly snoring away. He decided not to wake them. From the looks of the sheets from a legal pad and some ruled for musical composition that were strewn around the room, the two had put in a late night of working on music.

The click of the door upon Raif's departure woke the rock artist, Sam the Snake Sterling. His hands starting roaming Ted's body, which slowly brought Ted to semiconsciousness and led to Ted's hands roaming too. Quickly hard, Sam laced a forearm under Ted's right leg and raised it. In response Ted rolled up his pelvis, and Sam, going into a Spoons fuck, entered Ted's ass with his cock and started a slow, deep pump. While he fucked, Sam was humming.

"What's that you're humming?" Ted said, suddenly awake.

"I don't know. Was I humming? I guess I am just happy. I hum when I'm happy."

"That's it. That's the tune we've been reaching for. Quickly, get that on paper. I think you've got it." Oblivious to the fact that they had been having sex and were not that far from mutual ejaculations, Ted was rolling away from Sam and putting his feet on the floor.

"You mean *we've* got it. The tune is as much as yours as it is mine." Sam rolled in the other direction on the bed and sat up on the side, reaching for his briefs.

"I just thought of the lyric rhyme there in the second verse that had us stymied," Ted said, reaching for one of the stray legal pad pages and a pencil. "Get the tune on paper before it eludes us."

The two were deep into working on their song. If someone had mentioned to them that they were having sex just a few minutes earlier, they would have given that someone a blank stare.

Tim Cook Office, 10:30 a.m.

The breakfast service over, Sean had gone to the office and was standing outside the office door at the reception desk, his eyes taking in that no one was at the reception desk. Jeff Stockdon hadn't shown up for work yet. Sean hadn't noticed that before he'd come out to the reception desk to call up to the Alexander the Great Suite. Derek Hillsman hadn't turned up for breakfast. There was no answer in his room, either.

As he set the phone down, perplexed both that Hillsman hadn't answered and Stockdon wasn't here on duty, Val showed up at the desk.

"Did you know that there's a white kid giving a big black guy a blow job in a convertible in the parking lot?" She and Brad had gone straight upstairs to start servicing the rooms after they'd served breakfast. It was a big turnover day in the rooms.

"Is the car parked against the far wall?" Sean asked, his mind really elsewhere.

"Yes, it is."

"Then let's let it be. The neighbors can't see it. Bigger problems here. Have you seen Jeff Stockdon this morning?"

"No, sir. Oh, and Ricky is up and about and helping to change the rooms."

"Good. That means Brad isn't needed up there. Could you tell him to come down here after he's finished working on the rooms? Maybe he can hold down the reception desk until we get Jeff sorted out."

Alex appeared at the reception desk as Val left. He was euphoric from another successful food service.

"Jeff hasn't come in yet. We'd better—"

"In the office. In the office now," Alex growled. As soon as they were in the office and Alex had kicked the door shut, he grabbed Sean in his arms and began kissing him passionately. Sean was caught completely by surprised, but Alex wasn't the passionate kiss type and Sean was. Sean went with the kissing immediately. And with the fondling. And, with Sean pushed up to the back edge of the office desk, with his buttocks on the edge of the top, Sean went with the readjustment of clothing and met Alex' fumbling of stripping Sean's trousers and briefs off with unzipping Alex and hand-stroking his already-erect cock.

In no time Alex had his cock in Sean's passage, and an arm under the small of Sean's back, arching his torso back, while still kissing his mouth and throat.

123

Thrust. I want you so bad. Thrust. Does Eddie do this to you? Thrust. Thrust. Can Eddie pull groans like this out of you? Thrust. Thrust. Thrust. "Am I better than Eddie."

Alex had no idea he'd spoken the last until, in whimpery voice, Sean whispered, "Shit. Fuck. Oh, god yes, you're better than Eddie is."

They were frozen by the sound of the bell on the reception desk outside.

"Oh, shit. I've got to attend to that," Sean said, sitting up and gently pushing Alex away from him. "Guests are leaving and Jeff's not here."

"Jeff's not here?" Alex seemed bewildered, not least because he had been about ready to blow and had been cold cocked.

"No, and someone has to man the desk. It's turnover time."

"What if Jeff doesn't show up? He's flighty."

"I've asked for Brad to come down and pick up the duties. Ricky is up and about now, according to Val. Brad wants a job. I sense that you want Brad as part of our services here—as much as I do. If Jeff doesn't show up, there's a spot for Brad."

"Suits me," Alex answered.

A smiling Cory Townsend was at the desk.

"I hope you had a good stay, Mr. Townsend," Sean said. "And I hope the special service laid on was to your satisfaction."

"Yes, it was quite satisfying," Cory answered. "I'll recommend it highly. And I'll be back."

Townsend was followed by Mel Duncan.

"I'd like to book again for the second weekend next month," Duncan said during his checkout. "But I want to ensure it's a weekend when Brad Taggert is on duty."

"I'm sure it will be," Sean answered, marking in his mind to somehow hire Brad even if Jeff came back. "And I'll inform you if Brad won't be here that week."

Checking out next, together, and quite clearly together beyond that, were the rock star, Sam Sterling, and the pro tennis player, Ted Landon.

Landon was all grins and smiles. "Snake is going to let me be in his entourage for a two-week West Coast concert tour starting Friday. Isn't that great? We're working on a couple of songs together. He says he'll include any we finish in the concerts. I don't have another tournament for four weeks. Isn't that all great?"

"Yes, that's great," Sean acknowledged. Just looking at the two showed that they'd be very close during that concert tour and that maybe we wouldn't be seeing Ted Landon on the tennis tour again anytime soon—if ever.

"Yes, may I help you?" Sean asked of the two men—polar opposites—who appeared at the desk while Sterling and Landon were walking out, arm in arm. The big man was a black bull. Big was the word for him, heavily muscular, thuggish looking, and a bulge between his legs that would make a shy queer faint. The other one, on the other hand, was short, not more than five and a half feet, dark-haired and sultry—a fine slender body— and young enough that the first thought Sean had was "Two forms of identification for this one." He also assumed he knew who Val had been talking about concerning a white guy sucking off a black guy in a car in the parking lot.

"Do you rent rooms by the hour?" the black bull asked.

"We aren't really that sort of—" Sean started to say.

"That would be $50 by the hour," Alex broke in, extending his hand with a key in it. "Money up front. We

125

have to change all the linens like it would be a full-day rental. If you want it, it's the Harvey Milk Room, second floor, to the left, the middle room. A little cramped and just a shower bath, but if all you need is the bed . . ."

The black bull already had his wallet and $50 out.

"You will have to show two forms of ID with photo and birth date, I'm afraid," Sean said to the young white guy—after giving a dirty look Alex' way.

That done, the black bull pawed the young white guy up the staircase.

"That room is reserved for tonight," Sean said admonishingly to Alex. This was not the time or place for he and Alex to have a management discussion about going full brothel by renting rooms by the hour for sex, but Sean could see that they'd have to discuss it. Sean could arrange for only so much protection from scrutiny.

"The place is booked tonight?"

"Yes. The movie crew on second floor and a university men's swimming team from Clarksville University on the third floor."

"A men's team booked into a gay male B&B?"

"Yes."

Alex whistled. "There's going to be a whole lot of athletic fucking going on in here tonight. That's my kind of sex. I wonder how long it will take that porn movie director, Hal Burton, to come up with the idea of an orgy swim team movie, using all of the extreme Kama Sutra positions."

"And you'll see if you can go through the whole swim team during the filming?" Sean asked with a tight little smile.

"Depends. Eddie coming over tonight?"

"Not that I know of."

"Then no swim team for me. I'll be diving into you all night."

Sean's answering smile was a whole lot less frosty.

Harvey Milk Room, 10:10 a.m.

Both naked and on the bed, Chris Clarke, small, lithe, dark and sultry, a Mediterranean type, was doing a Crab on the big black bull with the thick nine incher. BBB was on his back, and Chris, face up to the ceiling, was hovered over him, hands extending behind and down, with the palms pressing into the hollow of the BBB's shoulders. Chris' feet were planted on the BBB's meaty thighs, and Chris was raising and lowering his ass on a cock that seemed almost an impossibility to be inside the young man's hole—but it was, a good seven inches deep at the deepest, as the rentboy fucked himself and moaned in tones he knew the john would appreciate.

And it was a nice room to fuck in. Chris was glad the BBB had brought him here rather than to a sleazy motel. It put him in a so much better fucking mood.

First Floor Ladies Room, 10:15 a.m.

Having time for a quickie before showing up to the swimming pool to start putting together his pool party orgy scene, Hal Burton was doing his own retake of the Suspended Congress scene with Val against the stall door of the ladies washroom. He and Val were getting very close. She hadn't left his room or his bed or having him inside her until slightly before she had to appear to help put final touches on the breakfast service.

This time Burton was back to the stall door, standing steady, cupping, squeezing, and spreading Val's butt cheeks, while she gripped the top of the stall door on either side of his head with her hands, had her feet planted in the stall door on either side of him at the level of his chest, and bounced her ass up and done on his cock.

For a neophyte Val was a very faster learner.

Harvey Milk Room, 10:25 a.m.

The big black bull and Chris were doing it in a Mastery position, with the BBB sitting on the side of the bed, legs spread and feet flat on the floor, with the rentboy in his lap, facing him. One of the BBB's hands was palming the small of Chris' back to keep the young man's body from launching away and the other was stroking Chris' cock hard. Chris was gripping the BBB's bulging left bicep with his right hand and had his left hand cupping BBB's neck. The BBB was giving Chris all nine thick inches and both of their pelvises were churning. They were bucking at each other like they were in a rodeo.

At 10:32, Chris let out a little cry, and his cream spouted as high as the BBB's chin.

Greg Louganis Pool House, 10:30 a.m.

Raif checked in with the movie company's clerk, Hanyu Li, who looked at him appreciatively but sniffed and turned up his nose. Li was a bit contemptuous of the amateurs Burton hired on location to fill out his movie casts.

"I see that Mr. Burton signed you at a premium. Are you any good?"

Before Li knew it, Raif had him stripped and in an Elevated Bodyguard position, with Li bent over the massage table, his fists pressing into the surface of the table, and his legs spread and Raif behind, a beefy forearm around his neck, pulling his head back for a kiss, while Raif mined his ass with his cock. After a couple of minutes of this, Raif pushed Li up onto the surface of the table and took him in a Pirate's Bounty, with Li flat on his back, right leg bent and spread, the ankle of the left leg hooked on Raif's right shoulder and Raif, on the table on his knees, gripping Li's neck with his left hand, pumping Li's ass with his cock, and firing off at will.

"You tell me," Raif said. "Am I any good?"

"The best," Li answered in a hushed voice.

At 10:50, Raif sauntered over to the swimming pool where the porn stars and cameramen were waiting, leaving Li a panting pile of satisfaction and belief on top of the massage table.

Harvey Milk Room, 10:50 a.m.

When the big black bull came, blasting the bulb of his condom with great gobs of cum, he was taking Chris in a Soaring Eagle, Chris on his back on the carpet at the foot of the bed, the small of his back running up the foot of the bed, and his legs suspended in air in the splits, while, clutching Chris' throat with one hand, the BBB's body, legs on the bed, other hand pressed in the carpet next to Chris' shoulder, fucked down into Chris' ass.

At 10: 55, the big black bull was gone, and Chris was sitting on the bed, counting twenty dollar bills, and looking around appreciably at the room. "I could live and have a ball being balled by guys in a room this nice," he said to no one in particular.

Tim Cook Office, 11:00 a.m.

Sean and Alex were at the reception desk, watching the big black bull hurry out of the door to the parking lot, and turning his head away as Detective-Lieutenant Pollack was entering the B&B.

"One of your employees, Jeff Stockdon, didn't come to work today," the cop said as he approached the reception desk.

"We know. That's why we're standing here," Sean answered. "We've been trying to call him and someone has to be here on duty."

"He doesn't answer his phone because I have him down at the station house. One of your guests, Derek Hillsman, isn't here, either."

"We know," Alex answered. Sean gripped his arm in warning, though. There was no reason for Pollack to know Hillsman's real name.

"That's because I have him down at the station too. Just thought I'd come and give you an update on the Jock Johnson death case."

Oh, lord, Sean thought. They already know his name too. "Have you charged these men with anything— Stockdon and Hillsman?" Sean asked.

"Stockdon, yes. Hillsman, no. He's been helping. Broke this wide open. It's murder—or maybe just manslaughter—Sean. I'll do what I can to keep it hushed up. Beardsley might be able to help minimize the media frenzy if he cooperates."

"Beardsley?" Alex asked, in shock.

"Yes, it seems Mr. Candidate killed his campaign manager. Looks like it might have been an accident, but there's the cover-up attempt to deal with. But, then, it's much easier for me to make a cover-up go away than a murder charge." He was giving Sean a meaningful look that wasn't wasted on Sean.

"So, what are the roles of Stockdon and Hillsman in it if Beardsley killed Johnson?" Alex asked.

"Hillsman put most of it together," Pollack answered, "And he came to me first thing this morning. The key was the timing. Johnson didn't die when we were led to believe he did. The coroner might have picked up on that, but he might not have looked for it and he might have given a timeframe that hid it. Johnson was dead— broke his neck from landing wrong when he was knocked down by Beardsley in a fight—before Hillsman went for his massage by Stockdon yesterday at 1:15 p.m. Lots of people heard the fight between Beardsley and Johnson.

They just didn't connect that with Johnson being found at the foot of the foyer stairs at 2:00 p.m. Turns out that Johnson died in Beardsley's room, not by falling down the stairs."

"And so?" Alex asked. This wasn't adding up for him yet.

"And so, first, Hillsman noticed that Beardsley took the massage appointment before his—at 12:30, when that was supposed to be Johnson's appointment, and Johnson didn't show up in Beardsley's 2:00 slot after Hillsman. He couldn't because he was already dead. And Beardsley took Johnson's massage slot so that he could leave for Toms River immediately after and no longer be in Cape May at the manufactured death time. And, beyond that, what brought it all together for Hillsman was when Stockdon left for several minutes in the middle of the massage, saying he needed more oil. Hillsman had seen an unopened bottle of oil in the pool house."

"So," Sean said, "Stockdon was suborned by Beardsley to change the time of death by taking the body from the Alexander the Great Suite and throwing it down the staircase sometime between 1:45 and 2:00, between the times Alex used the staircase."

"Bingo," Pollack said. "Your Mr. Hillsman will be back shortly to check out. I'm afraid your employee, Jeff Stockdon, isn't coming back. My guess is that it will be sold as an accident and that somehow the cover-up will all be swept under the rug as politically expedient."

"If it all goes away, what would Stockdon be charged with?" Sean asked.

"Theft," Pollack replied. "He was greedy. after tossing the body down the stairs, he went to Johnson's room and lifted the victim's watch and his wallet. We found them in Stockdon's duffel bag. He's lucky the chief doesn't want this publicized or we'd get Stockdon for murder. His oily fingerprints are all over the wallet and watch, and also on Johnson's belt and belt buckle, where Stockdon grasped the body to toss it. Good thing for us he was in the middle of giving massages with oil."

"But what did Beardsley have to offer him?" Alex asked.

"Money. It always comes down to money. Beardsley gave Stockdon a slug of money to clean up his accident. This is the main thing that's keeping the police chief happy with burying this one. The money will conveniently disappear. But it works to your benefit too. And it should work to my benefit also." He took a hard look at Sean.

"Is it all about money, David?" Sean asked Pollack. "Are you saying you want to be rewarded for your help with money."

"I think you know what I want, Sean," he said.

"Shall we go up to my bedroom?" Sean asked.

"Yeah, but I think I might like a little variety thrown in to this deal. You have some really cute guys on your payroll. That Ricky, for instance, is a real erection set."

"I'll see what we can do," Sean answered. "For now, I'll take care of the bill."

Although he knew why Sean was doing it and that it was for the benefit of both of them, Alex was still keyed up and a little resentful that Sean was waltzing off with someone else when the two of them had been interrupted in the middle of a fuck. That's why when he saw Derek Hillsman walking up the front steps from his morning at the police station, Alex came into the foyer.

"I heard you've had quite a morning," he said.

"Yes, I sure did."

"You did the right thing by telling the police all you know. You should be rewarded for that."

"And you might be interested in doing the right thing for me? You'll reward me?"

"You can see me as a reward?" Alex said.

"Need you ask that?" Derek responded.

"I'd be interested in doing you. Would you be interested in learning some new Kama Sutra positions?"

Sean's Bedroom in the Christopher Isherwood Suite, 11:30 a.m.

Wanting full value for the danger and trouble he was going through to bury the Beardsley case and the involvement of GayLords Inn in it, David Pollack fucked Sean to exhaustion, putting Sean in positions that stressed the innkeeper's muscles and forced him to do the heavy work.

Endeavoring to hold off in coming—by stopping the action and holding Sean immobile until the threat of ejaculation had passed and then moving on to the next strenuous position—Pollack managed to spin the session out to fifty minutes. The two men went from the Warrior position, with Pollack on his back, with his thighs raised and hooked over Sean's thighs, while Sean crouched over Pollack's pelvis and bounded up and down on Pollack's cock. From there they moved into the Warrior Reverse, with Sean crouched over Pollack's pelvis going in the other direction, holding Pollack's legs spread and raised by grabbing his ankles. Both positions were rough on Sean's hamstrings, but he soldiered on, knowing that the continued existence, even after three days of being open, dependent on Detective Pollack's favor and good will.

Pollack then moved Sean into a Fusion position, where Pollack was sitting on the bed, legs stretched out in front of him and spread, and Sean belly up, like in the Crab, had to straddle Pollack's pelvis with his legs bent, feet on the floor, arms stiff behind him, and his body raised. He had to put his ass on Pollack's cock and bounce on it. Taking over control, Pollack finished Sean and himself in a Soaring Eagle Reverse, where Sean was jackknifed with his thighs drawn up into his chest, his weight on his shoulders, and his butt in the air, facing the headboard, while Pollack was stretched over him straight bodied, arms extended down to the bed surface and feet hooked on the top of the headboard, while he did pushups on Sean's buttocks with his cock buried in Sean's hole. With his arms embracing his thighs, Sean grabbed his cock with his hands and masturbated himself to completion. Pollack kept doing pushups on him until he too shot his load.

Sean lay there stretched out on the bed, panting slowly and moaning quietly, with his legs spread, fighting cramps, and an arm draped over the side of the bed while Pollack took a quick shower, dried off in front of Sean, and dressed. Sean watched him the whole time. The man was hardbodied and hung. And a cruel streak ran through him not unlike Alex'. Sean realized he could have a much worse deal for protection.

"I can see that your operation here is going to be trouble," Pollack said, while he dressed. "I don't mind a challenge, but I expect to be rewarded for it."

"Yes, sir," Sean mumbled, knowing that Pollack expected to be treated as a master. He certainly was masterful with his cock.

"I want to know you or someone else who turns me on is available when I want it. I suggest that someone be free Mondays and Thursdays from five to six."

"Yes, sir."

"You turn me on, of course, and I fancy that Ricky Sanchez you have working here. When I want him . . ."

"Yes, sir."

"And if I bring someone here myself, there will be a room found for me for an hour or two."

"Yes, sir."

In contrast to Pollack, Alex took Derek Hillsman in six positions of no more than five minutes each and was finished and downstairs checking Hillsman out an hour before Sean managed to leave his room. Alex' purposes were two fold. First educational, to give Hillsman a flavor of male Kama Sutra positions—in this case all involving sideways fucks—and, second, he needed to get his rocks off—and relatively quickly.

Hillsman's primary purpose was to be masterfully fucked in new ways by the stud that was Alex. He also was keyed up and needed to get his rocks off too after a harrowing morning of giving his boss up—the candidate that he had been trying to get elected to the U.S. Senate. He certainly couldn't continue to work for Beardsley, knowing what he knew. He'd be driving straight to Washington, D.C., from here to start the search for a winning campaign to join from square one.

But for the next half hour, he was going to be willing putty in the hands of a master of sexual positions and of the deep fuck. He expected to be totally fucked and satiated.

And totally fucked he was, with Alex showing him nearly every way he could be sideways fucked in. They did the Scissors, with Derek on his back and Alex sideways to his body, with Alex' left leg bent on Derek's belly and Derek right leg hooked on Alex' leg and Alex sidesplitting him deep. Alex T-Squared Derek, with Derek folding his thighs up into his chest with his arms wrapped around them, and Alex on his side stretched out sideways below Derek, holding Derek's arm with his left hand and cupping his neck with his right hand as he fucked up into Derek's ass. And they did the Screw, with Derek on this back, his right leg thrown over his body, with his buttocks rolled up, and Alex kneeling beside him, pressing down on

Derek's right hip and his chest, and fucking him from the side.

Alex moved into the Doggy Twisted, with Derek on his belly, raised on his knees, with his butt in the air and Alex crouched over him from the side and fucking down into the hole. From there they went straight into a Side Rider, the sideways position for the Cowboy, with Alex on his back, palming the small of Derek's back with one hand and his belly with the other, as Derek crouched of him sideways and bounced on Alex' cock. Derek was finished in a flourish which brought Alex' load out of him too with an Overpass position, also known as the Pile Driver Sideways. This was the most taxing position for Derek of them all and brought the deepest groans out of him as well as an arc of cum. Derek lay on the bed, his weight on his shoulders and his legs arced over his torso, his arms stretched out straight above him, while Alex crouched over him on one side and fucked hard and vigorously down into his passage.

It was all quickly, athletically, and efficiently packed into a half hour with each transition immediate.

They showered together, with Alex giving Derek a surprise, slower, and more sensual Standing Bodyguard fuck from behind against the wet tiles of the shower while they were soaping each other up.

The Tim Cook Office, 12:30 p.m.

Derek Hillsman checked out, and with Brad Taggert present to start learning the job of the reception clerk, Alex was about to leave the reception desk and to plan out his breakfast menu for the next day. He had to feed both a randy porn movie crew and a swim team of university students. The fare would have to be more hearty than fancy. As he turned to leave, the rentboy, Chris, walked up to the desk, looking all sultry sexy.

"You still here?" Alex asked.

"We were done with the room on time," Chris answered, giving Alex a smile and a "come-on" look. "I heard them out at the pool when I came down and saw that a movie was being filmed. I was hired for a cameo. Making good money today, I must say."

"Good for you," Alex said, looking the young man over and feeling his insatiable dick hardening in approval of what he saw.

"Looks like you have a good operation here," Chris said. "Any interest in providing a room for an hourly rate arrangement?"

"You want to operate as a rentboy from this inn?" Alex asked. He didn't like beating around the bush. "Because if you do, we might be able to make an arrangement. We'd have to rake off most of the take, but you'd be getting a room and protection." Alex was aware that Sean was skittish about becoming a full brothel service, but Alex knew it was profitable and he was a risk taker. And Sean wasn't here at the moment.

"Yeah, maybe something could be worked out."

"Of course you'd have to audition first," Alex said and then looked at the young beauty expectantly.

"With you? Yeah, that would be fine. When?"

"Why not now?" Alex asked. "That's becoming the motto of GayLords Inn—no time like the present; who knows what tomorrow will bring?"

Chapter Five: Saturday, Two Months Later

The Basement of Eddie Renard's House on Benton, 3:30 a.m.

Chris Clarke, the rentboy based in the GayLords Inn, had shown curiosity about the basement in the Benton Street house of Eddie, Alex' brother, and a charter boat captain with big bones, huge muscles, and lots of flaming red hair. With both Eddie and Alex telling him what was down there, what Eddie used it for, and that there was a nasty side of Eddie, Chris' interest had only increased. He knew that Eddie regularly slept in the bed of Sean Temple, Alex Renard's partner in the B&B, and that the mornings after that Sean would be moving a bit slow and in sort of a daze. But having Alex in his bed had the same effect on Sean.

Chris wanted to try out what Sean was getting. Alex occasionally fucked him, and Alex was a master of positions. Chris wanted to know what Eddie was the master of, as Sean didn't seem to be able to make up his mind between the two.

He and Eddie were two hours into a bound and fuck session and Chris had already entertained two johns earlier in the evening. Still he was holding his own—and learning new things about this brother of Alex'.

Eddie had dressed for the occasion—black boots; black leather pants, leaving the buttocks and the cock and balls exposed; and a black leather harness criss-crossing his beefy and hairy chest. Chris was naked for the occasion. Chris was standing, but bent over double at the waist, belly into a wooden beam, with his back running out and down from the beam and his wrists tied off on either side of the beam. Standing behind him, hands on Chris' hips, Eddie was fucking Chris hard in the Bent Over position. When he was about to come, he pulled out and slapped Chris' rump a couple of times.

The urge to shoot having passed, Eddie moved Chris over to the black leather sling suspended from the ceiling by four chains. Making Chris bend over the sling, Eddie bound the rentboy's wrists to the chains at the head of the sling. He teased the young man's buttocks with the hard cock for a while, slapping the shaft on the butt cheeks, running it up the crack, and even pressing it to the hole without a condom on it, like he was going to bareback Chris. The rentboy moaned through this, wanting the cock again. "Do it, fuck me. Don't make me wait," he murmured.

Eddie laughed with surprise at how tough this young man was. Eddie specialized in breaking in young crew members of the charter boat fleet, reducing them to whimpering rag dolls in this basement. Chris had taken everything he'd done without breaking yet, and he was younger than a lot of the men Eddie broke in.

He didn't make Chris wait any longer. He worked his sheathed cock into the young man's hole, grabbed the chains on either side of the foot of the sling, and gave Chris the hardest, deepest thrusts he could, allowing himself to go to an ejaculation.

Chris hadn't come, though, Eddie untied his wrists and Chris just turned over into the sling, grasped his cock and slow stroked himself to his own load dumping.

While he did this, they talked a bit. "You OK with what you got?" Eddie asked. "You took it like a champ."

"It was intense," Chris said. "And different from what I usually get. It was good, yes. Fine."

"You going to let me do you again down here in a few days?"

"If you can afford it," Chris answered. "This was for me to try it out. The next time is business."

"If you want to try things out, I have a lot more of this you haven't seen."

"And maybe I'll see it if you can afford it."

"Cheeky little devil, aren't you?"

"I like you, Eddie—and I like what you do. I just can't give it away. It's my business."

"I can buy that. One thing, though, I want you to do—not to do, actually. Sean Temple doesn't do it to this level with me, and I don't want him to know how far I go with it—although I haven't gone too far with you with it yet." He gave Chris a menacing look, but Chris just smiled back at him. "So, I don't want you describing anything about this to him."

Chris didn't have any trouble agreeing to all of that, but it seemed a little unnecessary. Sean had seen this room the first night he'd met Alex, before they'd agreed to buy the B&B together. Sean knew what this equipment was used for.

"Do you bring other young men here?"

"Yes, there are many young men starting out at the marina who come down here."

"And what do you do with them? Do you put them on all of this equipment down here?"

"I bind them to whatever will break them," Eddie said in a low somewhat menacing voice. His face took on

140

a cruel aspect. "That's what I do. I break men. I make them into slaves."

"And what about Sean Temple? He somehow doesn't seem—"

"Sean has a sweet ass, and my brother is taken with him. No, I haven't put him on any of this equipment down here yet. We've just messed around with some toys in his room. I haven't broken him yet. But I will. Just as soon as Alex loses interest in him—or when I get tired of waiting for him. I'll break him and make him my slave, just like the others."

Chris shuddered. "What would you do to break me? I would like to be someone's slave—someone who took care of me."

"You're a tough little whore, but I could break you." Eddie already was rebinding Chris' wrists to the chains at the head of the sling and then his ankles to the chains at the foot of the sling.

"Oh, shit, yes! I'm a whore. punish me!" Chris was crying out and panting hard as Eddie was crushing his balls with one hand and had the fingers of the other hand up Chris' hole to the knuckles.

"So, am I going to have to pay for it from now on?" Eddie asked, with a sneer on his face.

"No, shit no, Eddie, you can do whatever you want with me. Just take care of me. Let me come."

The young rentboy was back in the B&B and in his bed in the Harvey Milk Room within the next hour. He smiled as he stretched and started to drift off to sleep. That had been quite a workout, he thought.

The Beach at the End of Decatur Street, 5:30 a.m.

Adam Vance came out of the surf and plopped down on his towel. It was still dark and the beach was deserted. He'd escaped New York earlier than he had planned, so he was here earlier than he could check in. He was taking advantage of the extra time by being alone with his thoughts and worries so that he could work them out. He'd never been pursued by a jealous psychopath before. It had been fun for a while but had gotten sort of creepy. Increasingly decisions were being taken out of his hands. He'd wanted to be the one to choose, but that wasn't being made possible.

He didn't even hear the figure steal up to him, grab him by the shoulders, and jerk him up to his feet. He didn't stay up long. He took a nasty jab to the mouth, followed by a strike into his solar plexus that took the wind out of his sails, and then an upper cut to his cheek that laid him out, flat on his back on the sand, and dazed.

His first thought was how stupid he was to be out here on the Cape May beach alone in the dark. He was being robbed and mugged. Instinctively, he reached for the duffel bag he'd brought that had both clothes and his wallet and watch in it. But he was backhanded flat on his back again, several feet from his duffel bag.

But the assailant didn't go after that. He was pulling Adam's Speedo off his legs, and it soon became obvious that his assailant was a man and wanted something more, or in addition to, Adam's money, because the man had a dick and it was inside Adam's ass canal. The man had him in a Bulldog embrace, with Adam on all fours and the assailant stand over his hips, the palm of his hands pressed into Adam's shoulder blades as he thrust his cock down into Adam's channel.

Adam bottomed for men, so having a man inside him wasn't the issue that had him almost hyperventilating. It was the surprise and violent domination of the man.

Adam was in a daze and he realized he could not win in a fight with this man. Adam was slim and elegant of body, smooth all over, and the muscles of the male fashion model that he was rather than pronounced muscles. The man was dark, very muscular, and matted with hair. The punches he had thrown had told Adam he had no chance against him. In addition, Adam knew this cock. He knew who this was—not just some transient mugger, but the boxing gym owner Adam had fled New York to escape.

He set his stance and moved his gaze to the surf rolling in just a few feet from him. He would endure this; he didn't want to anger him further. The man had a volatile temper to match his jealous possessives. The man grabbed the curly blond hair on the back of Adam's head and pulled his head back, painfully, arching his back, as the hard pumping continued.

After a few minutes of the Bulldog, the man collapsed Adam down on his belly into a Jockey Asian position, with the man crouched over Adam's hips, using the leverage of his feet to increase the vigor of his thrusts up into Adam's anal canal, and grabbing Adam's shoulders in his digging hands.

Adam was fully cowed—or certainly seemed so—when the man, who was barebacking him, pulled out, turned Adam over, shoved his legs under Adam's thighs, and pulled Adam's passage back onto his cock in a Sitting Bull position. The man stroked Adam's cock while he was pumping his ass. Adam, resigned, just lay back, his head toward the roar of the pounding surf and his arms; thrust out in supplication. Adam was brought to an ejaculation and soon thereafter the man creamed his insides deep.

"Want you to clean if off now," the man growled, the first sound beyond the man's grunts and Adam's moans and whimpers that had been made—which were drowned out by the roar of the surf to anyone not within a few yards of them.

As the man started to rise over Adam to bring his dripping cock to Adam's mouth, Adam gathered his strength and kicked the man in the nuts as hard as he could. The man rolled away from him, yelping and groaning and covering his privates with both of his hands, while Adam jumped up, grabbed his duffel, and raced off up the beach.

By the time the man had collected himself enough to pursue, Adam was across Beach Avenue and stumbling up Decatur Street.

At 6:00 a.m., Brad Taggert, the reservations clerk for the GayLords Inn was starting his day by coming out to the sidewalk for the collection of daily newspapers that would be put in the dining room for the breakfast service.

A naked young man fairly fell into his arms, dropping a duffel bag on the sidewalk. He was bruised about the face and torso and his thigh were scratched, but he otherwise looked very presentable to the discerning eye of Brad, who serviced guests' needs whether top or bottom. This one looked like a definite bottom.

"Are you OK?" Brad asked. "Are you hurt?"

"Must get off the street." The young man's voice was breathless, as if he'd run from across town. "Assaulted. He must not get to me. He'll kill me this time," Adam managed to get out the last, more dramatic points, out with a gasp.

"Quick, inside then," Brad said and helped the young man up the porch stairs and into the inn. "Here. We'll have to take care of these bruises and scratches and call the police."

"No police," Adam said with a panicked voice. "If they find him, he'll know how to get to me. He'll kill me."

"OK, no police then," Brad said. He'd come down just in a robe, and the robe brushed open at his chest as he held Adam and helped him move toward the reception desk. Brad, twenty-two, muscular, blond, and a bit thuggish, was also a hunk and a randy stud. Adam had the palm of a hand covering one of his pecs inside his robe, and this was having a warming effect on Brad. There was every evidence that Adam was warm in the same way.

"Now, where should we put you?" Brad said after he'd pulled the first aid kit out from underneath the reception desk and next went for the registration ledger. "What's your name?"

"Adam Vance. I'm from New York. I think I'm registered here for tonight."

"So you are," Brad said, surprised and giving Adam a questioning eye. The look turned into an assessing one, though. God, he's gorgeous; he could be a model, Brad thought—which, in fact, Adam was. Adam didn't miss the assessing look and, despite his predicament, and feeling safe now with this hunk of man, Adam was doing some assessing of his own.

"I left New York sooner than I anticipated and got here after I knew the inn would be closed," Adam said. "I decided to go out on the beach until morning. A bad move, I guess. I was assaulted."

"Assaulted? by a man? He didn't?"

"Yes, he did. But I'm not delicate. I let men fuck me. I know what kind of an inn GayLords is." He looked into Brad's face. That's how it is, he signaled with his eyes.

So, that's how it is; well, I can help you with that, Brad let pop up in his eyes.

"You're in the Brian Boitano Suite, third floor, front, on the left," Brad said. "If you'll let me dab at those wounds of yours, I'll take you up. Otherwise I'll give you the key and you can find it yourself. The room names are on the doors."

"I'd like you to take me up," Adam said. He knew this was exactly what had gotten him in trouble with his gym-owning boyfriend. He was too prone to having more than one boyfriend at a time. But he couldn't help it. This guy worked in a gay inn, he was a real hunk, and he wasn't backing off on possibilities.

After doing what he could and what little that needed to be done in cleaning Adam up and tending to his wounds—Adam hadn't covered himself and Brian hadn't suggested he do so. Adam was hard. So was Brian, and it was peeking out of the opening of his robe from time to time.

"Well, I'll just go now," Brian said, standing up from the side of the bed where they had both been sitting. "I have morning duties. Breakfast starts in an hour and a half, but it doesn't end until 9:30. You could get room service if you don't feel like coming down for breakfast."

"Would you be delivering the room service?"

"No," Brad laughed. "We have a couple of waiters. Gladly, that's not my job now."

Brad got up and moved to the door.

"You can leave the door unlocked," Adam said. "I don't mind if someone comes in."

"Perhaps then I shouldn't bother to go out at all," Brad said.

"Perhaps not."

Brad moved quickly back to the bed, sat, and pulled Adam into him. They went into a passionate kiss, and he reached for and grasped Adam's cock as Adam was untying the sash to Brad's robe and searching out Brad's cock.

Brad had Adam bent back on the bed with Brad's hand pushed between Adam's spread thighs and two fingers in his ass, when Adam asked him, in a whisper, "Should we be doing this? The hired help cavorting with the guests?"

"That's what we're here for—to cavort with the guests. This is a full-service inn," Brad said. "And now, unless you say you don't want me to—and with what you've been through, I could understand that you wouldn't want it, I'm going to fuck you."

"Cavort all you want," Adam whispered.

146

Brad gave him a gentle Leg Glider fuck, with Adam on his back at the foot of the bed, his right leg extending down to the floor and his left ankle hooked on Brad's right shoulder, his right hand latched onto Brad's left, the hand of which alternated between palming Adam's pecs and stroking his cock to an ejaculation. Brad remained deep inside Adam, moving his hips in and out, up and down, and in a revolving motion to kiss all of the walls of Adam's passage deep with the bulb of his cock.

Sighing and moaning, Adam was murmuring, "Yes, yes, fuck me. Fuck me harder. Harder!"

"Maybe tomorrow, if you want. Something to look forward to," Brad answered. "But you've been through enough tonight."

Sean's Bedroom in the Christopher Isherwood Suite, 6:30 a.m.

Sean lay pressed into Alex' chest, his legs splayed, an arm up and flung around Alex' neck, and his lips grinding on Alex' as Alex pumped his ass, finishing them both off, in Alex' favorite concluding position, the Pearly Gates. He had started with a more taxing Mastery, pulling a sleepy-eyed Sean over into his lap to ride his cock while he slapped and pulled Sean's butt cheeks apart to gain greater depth. For a few weeks now—with Eddie not visiting Sean's bed as much as possible, and Alex trying to curb his roving eye and dipping cock as well, he had endeavored to both end and start their day with an active fuck.

"Busy weekend?" Alex asked as they were cooling down, Sean still in the Pearly Gates position.

"Quite a few coming in, yes," Sean answered. "And Mel Duncan is already here—back in the Renée Richards Suite and, no doubt, with Brad in bed with him. That's what had brought him back—Brad. That was a good move of ours, hiring Brad to replace Jeff Stockdon. He's good and efficient—and the guests like him."

"And he's versatile. He'll fuck and be fucked. A great asset."

"I'm sure that's what's uppermost on your mind," Sean said, with a laugh. "He can be a crackerjack at the reception desk, but all you care about is how well he fucks the guests."

"Our reputation is going to be built on how well we fuck the guests. Evidence Mel Duncan coming back. It's not my food that brings him back. It's Brad's dick. And speaking of dick—"

"No you don't. You rightly brought up the topic of food. You have a breakfast to serve in an hour for the outgoing guests. And Hakim isn't quite as good at it as Val was."

"Yes, but Hakim gives a mean full-body massage, which means he replaces both Val, who ran off with that porn movie director, and Jeff Stockdon."

"The time is now 6:42," Sean said. "Hakim is probably in the kitchen, messing up who knows what, and you should be there too."

"Fuck it," Alex said, as he rolled out from underneath Sean and headed for the shower in his room on the other side of the Christopher Isherwood Suite.

The Renée Richards Suite, 6:42 a.m.

Brad opened the door to the suite quietly and looked over at the bed. It didn't look like the middle-aged managing director of a law firm, Mel Duncan, dragged out in his wig, Teddy, and red mesh stockings, had realized Brad had left him to bring in the newspapers and been gone longer than he anticipated. He dropped his robe and climbed up into the bed, spooning Duncan's body into his.

Brad was virile enough to be ready again, which was a good thing, because he was running on a tight schedule now with the unexpected early arrival of Adam Vance.

Brad moved a pillow under Mel's pelvis and repositioned his right leg bent over and up to give Brad's cock a target. Rising up on his knees and pressing a palm into Mel's belly, he slowly penetrated Mel's passage. Mel was coming awake, but it was in coos and sighs—and audible purring—Brad gently fucked him no deeper than rubbing the prostate. Mel wasn't a young man, and Brad had fucked him twice before they'd gone to sleep in each other's arms.

The Foyer, 7:55 a.m.

Brad brushed past a man on the grand staircase as Brad was going upstairs to check on the progress of the room cleaning. He stopped and did a double take and then went up the stairs more quickly. He found the young Hispanic waiter and room attendant, Ricky Sanchez, where he was afraid he'd be—in his own room, the Don Lemon Room. Ricky was putting his trousers on and the bed obviously had been mussed up. Ricky looked embarrassed.

"You were supposed to be in the dining room, serving a half hour ago." Brad admonished him.

"I know, but he wouldn't go until he'd fucked me again this morning."

"The man is from outside the inn. You asked me if you could use my room because you knew I'd be sleeping with the guest in the Renée Richards Suite?"

"Yes."

"Was that the same man who just left—who I met on the stairs down to the foyer?"

"Probably."

149

"Do you have any fuckin' idea who that man was?"

"No, should I?"

"Did he really fuck you?"

"Oh, boy, did he. He was like a rabbit. Surprised me for a man his age and size."

"OK, you'd better get downstairs and hope that Alex and Hakim don't tear your head off for being late."

The Tim Cook Office, 8:15 a.m.

Sean came down the stairs and approached the reception desk. Brad was there, looking none too happy.

"Something wrong, Brad?" Sean asked.

"The guest in the Brian Boitano Suite came in at 6:00 a.m.—I was out picking up the newspapers. He was assaulted on the beach and is a bit banged up. But he doesn't want to bring the police in it."

"Don't know how you managed that," Sean said, with admiration in his voice. "And you got him settled in?"

"Oh, yes, he's settled in all right. But that's not the real big problem."

"What is?"

"I let Ricky use my bedroom last night for an outside john. I was sleeping with Duncan. Seemed OK, but this morning I saw who the john was. He stayed all night."

"And?"

"It was the deputy mayor."

"Fuck," Sean exclaimed.

"It may not have been all that bad," Brad said. "I don't think it was a sting, which was my first fear—and yours, probably. Ricky said the man fucked him three times, including this morning. It sounds more like a move for a bribe than a sting."

"Shit. This business doesn't get any easier," Sean said. "I just managed to get the policeman, Pollack, sweet on both Chris and Ricky so he won't be at me all the time for protection dues, and now this. I told Alex that opening up to outside traffic and renting by the hour was going to come back to sting us in the ass."

On the Beach, 2:00 p.m.

"Don't worry, Joshua," Tony Taylor said. "I'm sure it's just a little angina. You'll be fine. Getting out of New York—away from that godawful play you're trying to save—will do wonders for you. And being here, in this gay-friendly inn will take us away from the questioning and judging eyes. A weekend here and you'll be able to straighten the kinks in that dreadful script."

"Well, I'm glad you didn't get a part in the play, Tony. I fear this one is going straight to the shelf rather than on Broadway."

The two men were sitting on large beach towels beside each other on the beach at the end of Decatur Street. They'd checked into the GayLords Inn early and come almost immediately out on the beach. The two men were quite a contrast. Tony Taylor, a young stage actor, a muscular and romantic young hunk stereotyped for the stage, was older than he looked—thirty-eight—and spent an inordinate amount of time in the gym to maintain that look. He was wearing just a Speedo and eying every man who walked by as if he were comparison shopping. He was good looking enough to get some speculative stares back.

Joshua Sinclair, in contrast, was wrapped in towels and wore a wide-brimmed straw hat to ward off the sun. He had a band of sun block across his nose and under his eyes too. It wouldn't be sunstroke he died from. He was sure that one of several other ailments, including ulcers,

151

would get him first. "Who gets ulcers in this day and age?" he asked himself, although he had done it aloud unwittingly. Used to such outbursts, Tony said nothing, knowing Sinclair would answer his question himself, which he did. "Producers of lousy Broadway-bound plays, that's who."

"Just relax and enjoy the vacation," Tony, Sinclair's much younger indulgence said. "In a bit we'll go back and take a nap before dinner."

A nap, to Sinclair, meant that Tony would fuck him. Truth be told, that's why he had Tony around. Joshua was still quite presentable for his age of sixty-one—tall, slim, standing erect, and an elegant speaker and dresser with a luminescent shock of white hair that covered his head in contrast to Tony's need to comb over a bit. It wouldn't be a very vigorous fuck, though. They were beyond that.

Besides, Joshua had never been sure that Tony was actively gay so much as actively thinking of a career that would benefit from fucking and sleeping with a Broadway producer.

"I'm ready for that nap now, I think," Joshua said.

"Ah, feeling randy are you?"

"Not so much as feeling sunburned and a little queasy."

The Tim Cook Office, 2:30 p.m.

"How are registrations coming?" Sean asked as he walked over to the reception desk after having dispensed welcome wine and beer in the Oscar Wilde Parlor to Mel Duncan of the Renée Richards Suite; a Jewish jeweler, the somewhat morose-acting Dieter Baum, of the Cole Porter Suite; and the two mismatched men from Broadway, Joshua Sinclair and Tony Taylor, registered to the Alexander the Great Suite. The new waiter, Hakim

Maroff, a dark Egyptian of large and perfectly proportioned musculature, who was the inn's full-body massager and power top in addition to waiter and room attendant, was passing around nibbles. Although Sinclair's eyes were on the more refined and handsome Sean, Duncan and Taylor were closely following the movements of the Egyptian stud giant. Baum was more interested in his drink.

It had only taken them a few minutes to learn that the late fifties Baum was recently bereaved, having lost his significantly younger partner, and was here for a bit of grief recovery and, if truth be known, some nookie. As he assessed Hakim as a top and that's what he was too, his interests were elsewhere. He had arrived around suppertime the previous night and had already engaged the submissive service of the resident rentboy, Chris Clarke. He hadn't taken long with Chris, though. All he wanted to do was to have a young, hard body under him for a quick ejaculation, and quick it had been. At his age, he didn't expect better or longer.

As Sean walked out toward the reception desk from the parlor, Alex was approaching through the Gore Vidal Dining Room.

"Uh, oh, here we go again," Alex muttered, as the front door opened and two, seemingly underage young men entered the foyer. They were shy with each other and each, in his own way, was a beauty. But they were in contrasting color. The blond was nearly an albino, very fair skinned and platinum hair offset with cornflower blue eyes. He had a nice smile, if diffident and a little skittish. The other guy with him was more solid, more muscular, a little rough looking, but beautiful of chocolate brown body. The platinum blond was dressed expensive preppy style. The black guy was in jeans and an athletic T. They both had luggage, the blond's from some upscale

153

department store; the black guy's probably from the Goodwill. But they seemed much taken with each other.

They also both seemed barely eighteen, if that.

"We're Scott Martinez and Tye Grant," the platinum blond said, stepping forward with a wallet in hand. It was evident he was paying the bill—that would have been evident just from looking at the two.

"Yes, certainly, Mr. Martinez," Brad said cheerily. "You're both in the Rock Hudson Suite. May I see two forms of ID with a photo and a birth date, please."

Grant showed signs of objecting, but Martinez obviously knew their ages were being questioned—and that they logically would be questioned. He pulled his ID out and gave a look of "we have to get through this to get what we want" at Grant, who shrugged and produced his, as well.

As the two went upstairs, Brad said, "Martinez just turned eighteen; Grant is nineteen. They give the same address in Princeton. I know the area. Multimillion-dollar mansions. Dollars to donuts Martinez is in the big house and Grant is in the servants' quarters. The same odds say their parents don't know they're here."

"Well, they won't hear it from me," Alex said, with some venom. "They're of age. They have a right to decide what they want to do and who they do it with."

Sean gave him a sharp look. There must be a story behind that. Maybe someday they'd be close enough—not just fuck close but friends close—for Alex to tell him what that was about.

It wasn't more than an hour later that this issue came up because another Martinez showed up, without a room reservation, but with an obviously open wallet. They gave the handsome and sexy forty-something-year-old Brazilian Felippe Martinez the Freddy Mercury Suite and also the demur that there was another Martinez and a dark-colored young man checked in.

"We'll have to do what we can to keep those separate," Alex said when Martinez climbed the stairs to his room.

"He's gay," Brad said. "He doesn't want anyone to know it, but he can be had—and probably hasn't had it so long he craves it. He can't accept that his son has similar interests now, but he just needs time—and to be laid real good."

"How can you tell that?" Sean asked.

"I can just tell," Brad answered. "I've had a lot of experience with guys who don't want to admit they want it but who melt when it's offered."

"So, offer, Brad," Alex said. "I'll work on the young guys and you mellow out the father. We'll just have to keep them apart until that's done."

"Don't you think that's really none of our—?" Sean started to say.

"It's the right thing to do for both sides," Alex said in a voice that would entertain no disagreement. "That's part of what we want to offer here—the lowering of barriers and the acceptance of who these men are and what they want. I have no doubt that those two young men want each other and are only suffering from a class and wealth barrier."

Sean pointed to the door to bring notice to another arrival. "This will be fun and games for sure," he said. Walking in from the parking lot side were three men: a middle-aged man of around fifty and not quite successfully trying to look thirty-five, although his musculature was fine, and two obvious boy toys, one on each side, pulled into the older man's sides.

"So, now we know," Brad said.

"Know what?" Alex queried.

"That would be Frank Hosler and two who he'd only identified as Kurt and Colin. They're in the Elton John Suite. I tried to tell him that it wasn't for more than two, but now I can see that they'll all be using the same bed."

After they'd checked in, Sean took them to the parlor, where he'd already loaded the Brazilian, and Alex returned to the kitchen to work on the dinner service.

One last, unexpected arrival transpired. But he didn't stay. The man, in his early thirties, tattooed and with a ponytail and looking a little rough, came up the front walk and into the inn.

"Hello, I'm looking for someone who might be registered here," he said. "A friend I'm trying to track down. His name is Adam Vance."

Brad stiffened and made like he was looking at the register. "No, sorry, no one by the name here."

"Well, maybe he'll check in later. Can I leave my card, with my cell phone number on it, to leave in case he shows up. It's important that I find him."

"Certainly, if you wish," Brad said somewhat stiffly, fighting the urge to lash out and pop the man one.

He watched the man leave up the walk; took a look at the card, which identified him as Neal Ehlers, and tossed the card in the trashcan. He didn't bother to look at the man's occupation. He probably should have.

Elton John Suite, 3:30 p.m.

The slightly tubby middle-aged grocery store chain owner, Frank Hosler, and his two ambitious late-teens twink grocery clerks, Kurt and Colin, were showing why one bed was quite big enough for three men. It all depended on how you stacked them. They moved from a Spit Roast position, where Colin was the centerpiece, on all fours on the bed, with Frank at his rear, on his knees, fucking him Doggy style, while holding Colin's hips in his hand. Kurt was kneeling at Colin's head, his cock being serviced by Colin's mouth.

Then it was Kurt's turn to be on Frank's cock in a Perfecta position, with Frank lying on the bed, his legs spread and reaching to the floor at the foot of the bed, with Kurt riding his cock in a Cowboy and Colin kneeling between Frank's thighs, sucking Frank's balls, and licking the section of the root of his cock that wasn't buried in Kurt's passage.

Frank was glad he'd found the B&B. He enjoyed these little weekend excursions to help him decide who to promote in his grocery stores. Both of these young men were vying for a section manager spot in their respective grocery stores and both were doing great in showing Frank good customer service skills.

Truman Capote Library, 3:30 p.m.

"Ah, here you are, sir. I brought you a brandy." Brad had found the Brazilian, Felippe Martinez, sitting on a sofa in the library. After handing the Brazilian the brandy, Brad sat down beside him. Martinez seemed a little nervous. "You say you came to Cape May looking for your son, but you didn't mention that your son is of age and gay. And you have checked in here too instead of some other hotel while you looked for your son. Isn't that telling us something? Aren't you gay too? Don't you wish to have a little action yourself?"

"Of course not," Martinez said indignantly.

"Is that really true? You were giving me looks I'm accustomed to when you were checking it. You seem nervous with me sitting here by you." He moved an arm around Martinez' back along the top of the sofa and touched Martinez' shoulder with his fingers. "And I can feel you tremble when I touch you. I can tell you're getting hard too." He reached over with his other hand and ran his fingers down Martinez' basket.

"Really. This is entirely too forward," Martinez said.

"And yet you're still sitting here. You're here the same as your son is—because you want something—something we can supply at this inn."

"My son is here and you know it? Is he with that . . . ?"

"With that black young man? Yes, he is. You can't say it because you don't approve of your son being actively gay, because he's fucking someone below his class, or because he's fucking with a black man?"

"Really. You go too far."

"Do I?" Brad had his hand palming and squeezing Martinez' package. "And yet you are still sitting here because you know you want to have sex with me." He turned and beckoned Chris Clark in. The rentboy came to the sofa and sat on the other side of Martinez. Chris laid a hand on Martinez' thigh and cupped the Brazilian's neck with the other one. "I asked if you objected to your son engaging in gay sex or that he does so with a black man—a young black man who is well built. I'll bet he's even hung. You are dark complexioned yourself, Mr. Martinez. Have you ever had sex with a black man?"

"Tye is the son of my grounds keeper," Martinez said.

"So it's a class thing. You don't care if your son has gay sex, you just don't want it to be with the hired help."

"Of course I care about that—that he would have gay sex." He was beginning to pant. Chris was unbuttoning his shirt.

"Your son is of age and you yourself engage in sex with men, don't you? And it gives you pleasure, doesn't it? You would deny the same pleasure to your son? I ask again, have you ever had sex with a black man?"

"Yes." It was like the answer was being torn out of him. Chris was unbuckling his belt buckle. Brad was unzipping his trousers. Martinez was doing nothing to counter them. He was panting and trembling.

"Someone of a lower class?"

"Yes, our chauffeur back in Sao Paulo."

"And he was good? You got pleasure out of his fucking?"

"Yes. But that's behind me now. I have responsibilities—and government clearances. I own a defense contracting company. I can't—"

"But I think you can, Felippe. You've come to an inn that is very gay friendly and tolerant. You are going to have sex here with Chris and me. You know you are. But it will be quite discreet. You will enjoy the fucking, and none of this will get back to your business. Just like your son, who is of age, has come here to enjoy himself discreetly with the lover he has chosen. No different, really, than a lover you have had yourself. You don't want to lose your son, do you?"

"No, of course not."

"Nor do you want your son to rebel against your opposition by flaunting his chosen lifestyle publically."

"No, I guess not."

"So, you will let him take the pleasure discreetly that he came here to take—being old enough to make that decision himself—and you will take your pleasure too. You do want Chris and me to fuck you, don't you?"

"Yes." again pulled out of him like a taffy pull.

"Tell me, Felippe, do you give cock or do you take cock?" Brad had Martinez' cock in his hand, and Chris was teasing the Brazilian's trousers off his legs.

"Yes, both," Martinez answered with a croak.

"How convenient," Brad said softly, turning Martinez' face to his to take him into a kiss as Chris bent over the Brazilian's lap and swallowed his cock.

They fucked in an Anal Train position, with Chris draped over the arm of the sofa; Felippe draped over

Chris' back, fucking him; and Brad covering Felippe, with his cock buried in Felippe's hole and controlling the thrusts of both himself and the Brazilian.

Chris left after the threesome was consummated, and Felippe, now fully energized, sat in Brad's lap in a Mastery Kneeling position, with Brad slouched on the sofa, with his legs spread and feet on the floor. Felippe, facing him, and with his arms behind him, hands on Brad's knees, rode Brad's cock hard.

Afterward, they lay stretched against each other on the sofa, kissing and fondling each other.

"There, how long have you denied that to yourself?" Brad asked.

"Too long," Felippe answered, with a sigh.

"You know you only need to come back here to enjoy a very private blowing out of your pipes. And don't you think your son deserves that joy too—with whoever he wants to be with here?"

"I suppose."

"You can accept it? He and the black groundskeeper's son—like you and the black chauffeur?"

"Yes, I think I can."

"We can test that. I've made an appointment for you for a full body massage in the pool house. We can go out there from here."

"How does that test my acceptance of my son's choices?"

"Scott and Tye are at the pool. I'm sure they are fucking—maybe even getting instruction in high-quality fucking. They seemed to be a little nervous and confused when they checked in. You'll be able to see them fucking while you get your massage."

"I think I can manage that."

"And, oh yes, the masseur is a black Egyptian with a supersized black cock. His full-body massage will

160

include fucking you hard with a jet-black cock. Can you take that?"

"Yes."

"And afterward I'll take you up to your room and fuck you into dinner time."

"I think I can manage that too." Martinez was sounding nearly so nervous and disapproving now.

Tim Cook Office, 3:45 p.m.

"What can we do for you, Mr. Deputy Mayor?"

Edwin MacAlister was sitting on the other side of the desk from Sean at the B&B office.

"I think there may be a problem with your business that I would like to go over with you before I take it to the council."

"And you thought you should come here in person to discuss it with me rather than calling on the phone or going straight to the council?" Sean asked, leaning forward over the desk and giving the city official a sharp look.

"I don't know what you mean by that," MacAlister said.

"Let's cut directly to the chase, Edwin. I can call you Edwin, can't I, since it looks like we'll be doing business with each other?"

"I don't know what you mean by that either," MacAlister said, but he was beginning to look a little uncomfortable.

"This is some sort of shakedown, isn't it Edwin? Let's be honest and direct and get these negotiations over. You want something to not report us. I'm willing to give you something for going beyond that and helping to protect us. I don't think you want money. Our employee, Ricky Sanchez, said you spent the night here last night and fucked him three times. You might be interested to know that he said you were good at it. That sort of neutralizes the leverage you have. You tell the council we're operating a house of ill repute here, and I tell them you availed yourself of one of my employees sexually—three times. If you wanted to establish what could be gotten here, you didn't need to establish it three times."

"Well, I suppose there could be an arrangement of some sort." The deputy mayor was decidedly uncomfortable now.

"You enjoyed Ricky, didn't you? You enjoyed him three times."

"Yes."

Sean got on the intercom and traced Ricky down, who appeared at the office door.

"Did this man treat you as you would like last night?" Sean asked him.

Ricky looked shyly from one man to the other.

"Yes, sir, he did."

"Would you mind servicing him a couple of times a week? This is entirely up to you."

"No, I wouldn't mind," Ricky answered.

"You can have an hour each on Mondays and Wednesdays; another official has taken Tuesdays and Thursdays. I don't mind telling you there is another official in on this. It will give you second thoughts about screwing around with us. If you do, I'll tell him you are protecting us too. Do we have a deal?"

"Yes," MacAlister answered.

"Do you want to seal the deal now with Ricky?"

"Yes."

"What did this man like best, Ricky?"

"I think he liked sucking my dick best." MacAlister nodded his head.

Sean called in Raif, and the mere presence of the hunky Jamaican handyman with the dreadlocks seemed to make the deputy mayor salivate.

"Raif, I think this man would enjoy sucking two cocks at once. Could you take him and Ricky to your room and give him a 369 and a Double Header? And then leave him with Ricky to do what he wants. He's going to be a regular client from now on."

Both the 369, involving Ricky and Raif kneeling on the bed with their cocks close together and MacAlister working at stuffing them in his mouth at the same time, and the Double Header, which had Ricky and Raif lying on their backs, their legs over each other and their cocks together, with MacAlister sitting beside them and taking both cocks in his mouth, involved the deputy mayor and two cocks at once. When Raif was gone, MacAlister got himself off by putting Ricky in a Pyramid, a form of a Missionary position, Ricky on his back on the bed, legs thrown over his shoulder, and MacAlister crouched over his midsection, fucking down into his passage.

While this was transpiring in the Diesel Washington Room, Eddie Renard and Chris Clarke were approaching the reception desk. Eddie dinged the bell, and Sean came out of the office. He knew that Brad was otherwise engaged with the Brazilian in the library. Chris Clarke was carrying two suitcases.

"Yes? It looks like you're moving on, Chris," Sean said. He wasn't all that disappointed. He'd kept saying that giving an outside rentboy status in the house was a bad idea.

"Yes, he's decided to move in with me," Eddie answered for Chris.

"Has he now?" Sean said. For some reason he had the strong feeling that this marked a watershed—that Eddie wouldn't be visiting him at night again. He hadn't done so for nearly three weeks. Sean felt relief without really knowing why, although he'd never been quite sure about Eddie—and his sleeping with Eddie seemed to have visibly rankled Alex, Eddie's brother. Maybe this was all for the best.

"Yes, I'm going with Eddie," Chris said. He so wanted to let Sean know that he probably was saving Sean in the process, but he wasn't really being all that noble. Chris did want the excitement that Eddie was promising him. Chris, as a rentboy, had become jaded in what excited him.

The Swimming Pool Area, 4:00 p.m.

Alex walked around the swimming pool and to the row of lounge beds running in a line down the side of the pool. Picking one that was beside the bed where Tye Grant was front-to-front on top of Scott Martinez, Scott's legs spread, with Tye between them, and squirming around on top, Alex sat down, legs spread, facing them.

Slapping Tye on the bare buttocks, Alex cheerily said, "In yet? You boys have been doing a lot of wrestling around on top of each other, but I don't see that you've gotten very far. Got your dick in him yet?"

The two young men looked up at Alex, eyes startled. Tye started a "Fuck you" response, but saw that it was one of the owners of the B&B, and he went into his trained, respectful "don't talk back" stance.

"We're working on it; he's too big," Scott whimpered from underneath Tye.

"He's had time to take you for a joy ride if you guys were trained to do it right with each other. Here, let's see how big he is. Sit up."

The two young men dutifully parted and went up in cross-legged position, facing Alex.

"Yes, he does have a beauty," Alex said, as he cupped Tye's erection in one hand and Scott's in the other. "I can see why you like him. How long are you, Tye?"

164

"Eight inches," Tye responded hesitatingly.

"Looks more like seven and a half, but quite thick. And you, Scott, yours is very nice too. And both are getting harder. Why is that, guys? You've been bumping and grinding for twenty minutes out here. Why is that you can grow bigger in my hands?"

Neither answered; they both looked a little bewildered.

"It's because of the excitement of something different and strange," Alex said. "Listen, you two came here, paying big bucks to do so, to have exciting fucks. You're both athletes, aren't you?"

"Tye's football and I'm track. At different schools, naturally."

"Naturally," Alex said. He didn't have to be told that Scott had gone to a prep high school and Tye to a public one.

"And you're both hunks, young, and I assume virile. You both also are hot for each other," he said. "What you need is training and spice. Tell me, Tye, have you ever yet been able to get all of this monster cock inside Scott?"

"Uh, I'm really too big for him."

"No, you're not—and both of you will reach new heights of arousal, pleasure, and satisfaction when you do. If you like, I'll step you through some ways to make the most of your pleasure weekend here. You could be—and should be—fucking like pros. If you don't want some help, just get up and leave."

Neither one of them moved. They both had quizzical looks on their faces, but Alex could tell by the throbbing of the two erections he held in his hands that they both very much wanted what he was offering. He took his hands away, and said, "First, more effective and arousing preparation, then on to these." He pulled a pile of Trojan Magnums out of the pocket of his gym shorts.

165

Scott blushed and Tye said, "We've only been with each other. We don't use those."

"Even better for the height of pleasure," Alex said, not admonishing or lecturing them but only suggesting. "Still, you should both have a supply handy. You may want to experiment with others—and, if you do and you both accept it, don't feel guilty about doing it. Sex is sex and sometimes variety helps enhance your times together with each other."

"So, how do you prepare? Do you 69?"

"Yeah, sometimes."

"Do you eat each other out, suck balls, lick armpits, finger fuck, use poppers?"

He got blank stares.

"What are poppers?" Scott asked.

"Here, take a whiff of this." Alex opened a popper bottle and waved it under Scott's nose. "Whiffs of this when Tye is trying to get inside you will calm you, help with the pain, and will relax your channel muscles so you can open more to him."

"All of that, really?" Scott asked.

"Yes, all of that . . . really. You just have to be careful how much you sniff. The point is for Scott to be open enough to take you so that you slide right in when the time for fucking comes, Tye. The foreplay is important. There are exotic forms of 69 that will send Scott right through the roof of lust and have him open and begging for you. You're both young, muscular, flexible, and athletic. And you seem to be hot for each other. We'll start with the Standing 69. I'll bet you've only done it lying one on top of the other. Let's spice it up. Stand up on the stones, Tye. Yes, like that. You're a big, strapping son-of-a-bitch, aren't you? Now pick Scott up and spin him around so his legs go over your shoulder and you can suck him and he can suck you. Yes, like that. More arousing than any 69 you two have done before, isn't it? Now, roll Scott's buttocks over and eat his ass out. Tongue him. Get him opened up more. There, don't you love the sound of his moaning?"

After a few minutes of this, Alex said, "OK, give him a thrill. Make him fly over you. This is called the Plumber. Go on your back, Tye, on the lounge bed, feet on floor to give you strength and steady you. Make Scott fly over you in reverse. Raise him over your head with his legs spread and you holding his thighs up and out. Keep yourself straight in the air, Scott, with your hands on Tye's head. Now you face fuck Tye, while Tye sucks you to an ejaculation. There, isn't that exciting?"

Alex helped to get the two go back onto the bed in a half recline, Tye behind Scott and embracing him. "Scott needs to be real open for that cock of yours Tye. Bend and push his leg up into his chest. Yes, like that. Roll his buttocks over. Lean your head down and suck on his hole. Here. Take a whiff of this popper, Scott. Yes, like that. Hear him moan and beg for it, Tye? Now, get your middle finger in there. Slowly, as you can, stretch him until you can get three fingers in him and easily slide them in and out. Use this lube here or your spit, or both. Talk dirty to him as you do. Excite him. Make him beg for the cock. Roll him over on his back now and work your cock inside him. There, he's more open than he's ever been before, isn't he? Now slowly feed him all of it. Stop when it's too tight and give him a few moments to stretch to you. He'll do that. His moaning and groaning tells you he wants to do that. He wants all of you. Let nature do its thing. Then keep pressing until he has it all. Slow pump him now, always returning to where your curly pubic hairs are mingling with his. Don't come, though. Pull out before you can't control the urge. We have more positions to go to. The more positions you can do in a fuck, the higher your arousal will go, the more cum you will spout."

After a few minutes. "There, he should be able to take you in exotic positions now. He wants all of you. We're going to get all of you in there each time, and you both are going to heaven. You're both young and strong, and Tye is big enough to support Scott. You two can be having a ball fucking when you learn to be skilled and inventive. Let's try an athletic version of the Cowboy Asian. Take a bit of a rest, Tye. You deserve it. Time for you to work, Scott. Tye, put your butt on the edge of the sunbed, your torso down to the floor, your arms bent and knuckles on the stone to steady you. Now you, Scott, sit on the cock and fuck yourself, crouched over Tye's hips and facing his arched-back torso. Support your torso by leaning a bit forward, with elbows on knees. Now fuck yourself on his cock. Don't let him come yet, though. I'll show you one more position after this."

Alex moved them into a Reverse Pile Driver, with Scott taking his weight on his shoulders, his arms thrust out to the side, his torso reaching for the ceiling and his buttocks over his face, while Tye crouched, standing, over him, Scott's ankles on Tye's thighs, and Tye fucking down, deep into Scott's now-flaring hole.

As the two lay in each other's arms on the lounge bed, both panting, both having achieved a satiating ejaculation, and both looking appreciably at Alex, the B&B owner slapped Tye on the rump again. "There, that's a start. The two of you are going to make great sex with each other. Before I leave, I'll give you the URL on a gay male Kama Sutra sex positions Web site you can consult and try out positions from. Remember, keep it exciting and spicy and you'll get all of the satisfaction out of a fuck that you could imagine getting."

At the end of the pool, in the open-sided pool house, nothing that was happening between his son and his groundskeeper's son at the pool was being lost to

Felippe Martinez, who was getting a full-body massage from the big, black Egyptian, Hakim Maroff.

He was well past mellow in Hakim's manipulation of his body and the two ejaculations he'd already had. He didn't have the energy to do more than look on what the young men were doing with interest. At that point he was on top of a stretched-out Hakim, his arms flung back, fists buried in the hollow of Hakim's shoulders, his legs bent, his feet on Hakim's thighs, and he was fucking himself on Hakim's thick, jet-black cock in the Bent Spoon positions.

The Foyer and Front Sidewalk, 4:15 p.m.

Having turned the Brazilian, Felippe, over to the magic hands and cock of Hakim, Brad returned to the reception desk to ensure all was in order and to take care of the reservations having come in by e-mail. He heard a clatter on the stairs and came around to the door to the foyer to be able to catch sight of the assaulted young man of the night before, Adam Vance, tripping down the stairs and bursting out of the front door, yelling a squealed "Neal!"

Vance hadn't appeared for breakfast or gone out for lunch that Brad could figure. Brad had just thought that the young man was in too much pain from his injuries the night before—and maybe the effects of Brad fucking him afterward—to leave his room. It also occurred to Brad that Vance was hiding from his assailant. Brad hadn't told him yet about the man, presumably the assailant, who had come looking for him earlier in the day.

Brad went over to the front door to see what had brought Vance out of his room—to see that he was on the sidewalk and in the embrace of the very guy who had come looking for him earlier. Brad quickly returned to the reception desk to retrieve a short bat he kept there for insurance and then walked deliberately through the foyer and front door and down the porch steps. The nearer he got to the pair the more obvious it was that Vance wasn't in danger. He was draped all over the man.

Turning and seeing Brad, Vance smiled and said, "This is my boyfriend, Neal Ehlers. Isn't he gorgeous? I saw him on the sidewalk from the window of my room and waved to him and came right down."

"Yes, he is gorgeous, but I thought you had some trouble with your boyfriend last night," Brad said. He'd lowered the, bat but Neal Ehlers was still nervously eyeing it.

"Was Stan Brown here last night?" Ehlers ask, now looking at Vance. "Did he assault you? Is that what these cuts and bruises are about, Adam?"

Damn straight he assaulted Adam, Brad thought, right before I fucked him. And now Adam is draped all you. Brad was beginning to think that Adam Vance was a bit of a flake.

"Yes, but he's gone now, baby," Vance cooed at the man standing and holding him tight on the sidewalk. "And he'll have a couple of months to cool off. He'll forget all about me and move on to someone else to shove around."

"Oh, do you have reason to believe he was arrested last night for lewd behavior?" Brad asked. "And what's going to keep him away from you for a couple of months?"

"I called the gym in New York earlier this afternoon," Vance answered. "I asked for him and when he came on the line, I hung up. So, he's back in the city now. And I'll be in Europe the next couple of months. That's why Neal was trying to track me down. He's a fashion photographer. He's taking me to Europe with him and I'll be doing photo shoots for men's cologne ads. Isn't that simply divine?"

"Yes, simply divine," Brad answered, trying to put a little enthusiasm into his voice. "If you'll excuse me, I have to get back to the reception desk."

"Do you mind if Neal spends the rest of the weekend in my room?" Adam asked.

"Sure, no problem. I have his card somewhere. I'll add him to the register." The "somewhere" Brad had Neal Ehlers card was the trashcan—he now knew he should have read the card, which would have identified him as a fashion photographer, not the gym owner Vance had said he escaped from. The trash hadn't been taken out yet; he could retrieve the card. They rented by the room. As long as anyone else was registered—or very discreet—they didn't care if there were extra people in the room.

"Oh, and you were really good to me last night, Brad, maybe—"

"He was good to you last night?" Neal asked, suddenly interested in the conversation.

"Yes, he dressed my wounds and scratches."

"Oh. That was nice of him."

"And he fucked really, really good too."

Brad expected an explosion, but what he saw in Neal's eyes was interest instead. Neal had a good body, especially if you liked a full display of tattoos, and his face would be handsome enough with his ponytail undone and his reddish-brown hair framing it. Nice soft mouth. Good for blow jobs.

"Neal and I like . . . well, company is good," Adam said. "Maybe if you're not busy later tonight . . ."

"Maybe," Brad answered.

The Alexander the Great Suite, 4:45 p.m.

"I'll be gentle with you, baby. I know you aren't feeling the greatest. But maybe you just don't want—"

"I want you inside me," Joshua Sinclair murmured to his younger lover, Tony Taylor. "I've waited all day for you to be inside me, and that's what we came to the B&B for this weekend to do."

"Well, OK, if you're sure. How about a Seesaw, then? It won't be too strenuous for you."

"Yes, whatever we can do. Whatever position you can use to bring us off together. You know how much I love that."

"Sit up on the bed then."

Taylor, in magnificent musculature, spending hours a day when he could in the gym in working to maintain a body that made women—and many men—swoon when they saw him on stage, climbed up on the bed and moved to the center, sitting with his legs extended straight out. Sinclair, naked, and in very good condition for a sixty-one-year-old man who claimed several ailments, gingerly came up on the bed and lowered himself in Taylor's lap, skewering his ass channel, with Taylor's help, on Taylor's cock. Sinclair's legs encased Taylor's hips. The two men went into a prolonged kiss, and Taylor wrapped an arm around Sinclair's back. His other hand went between them, grasped Sinclair's cock, and stroked it to the rhythm of the rocking motion Taylor set.

The two men rocked together for some fifteen minutes, while they kissed and Taylor stroked Sinclair's cock. The rocking became more rapid and vigorous, and the two men were panting and groaning.

"Are you close?" Taylor asked with a gasp. "I am."

"I can come once you start," Sinclair answered, his voice labored by his heavy panting.

"Fuck, shit, Joshua," Taylor cried out in a strangled voice. "Here it comes!"

"Seed me baby!" Sinclair exclaimed.

The two tensed and held for a nanosecond. And then they each jerked and let out a long gasp. Once again the two had achieved the ultimate shared ejaculation.

Giving out a grunt and a long release of air, Taylor's body collapsed on Sinclair, pushing the older man onto his back.

"Tony? Tony, baby? You're too heavy for me. Roll to the side, please. Tony? Tony, honey. Tony, are you OK? Oh, God no, Tony!"

Joshua Sinclair was standing at the door of his third-floor suite, yelling, "Help! I need help! I think he's dead!" as Brad came running up from the reception desk; Raif from the kitchen, where he'd been working on a plumbing leak; and Sean from the second-floor Christopher Isherwood Suite.

Raif was faster than the rest and was in the room and back out while Brad and Sean were trying to get Sinclair calmed down enough to make sense. The jeweler in Cole Porter Suite on the same floor, Dieter Baum, also had come out to see what the screaming was about and then popped back in his room for a blanket to cover Sinclair with.

"Yep, the one in the room definitely is dead, mon," the Jamaican handyman declared as he came back out of the room.

"Here," Sean said, as Dieter came back with a blanket and wrapped it around Sinclair, who looked at him with uncertain, but grateful eyes. "Could you take Mr. Sinclair into your room until we can get this sorted out, Mr. Baum."

"Yes, of course. Come with me, Mr. Sinclair. We will comfort each other. I know exactly how this is."

"Brad, could you go call Dr. Overby and ask him to come over. The body . . . Mr. Taylor will need to be attended to. And Raif . . . Detective Pollack—"

"I could call him after calling the doctor," Brad said.

"He doesn't need to be called," Sean said. "He's down in the pool house getting a full-body massage from Hakim now—and he has a 5:00 p.m. appointment to fuck Ricky. He won't be pleased that this situation will have screwed that up."

Chapter Six: Later That Night

The Harvey Milk Room, 8:00 p.m.

Ricky Sanchez lay chest down on the bed, one arm outstretched with the hand of the other stroking his own cock to a soon-to-be-enjoyed ejaculation. His body was in languid motion, chest arching up and down slightly, rolling his forehead on the bed in sexual ecstasy, and butt slightly elevated and moving languidly back and forth and up and down on Dr. Overby's buried dick. The doctor, standing on the floor at the foot of the bed, covered Ricky's body from above. His arms were arched over Ricky's head, fists buried in the bed's coverlet, and he was licking Ricky's back and whispering sweet nothings to the young man. He had fucked Ricky in the Basset Hound position and had just filled the bulb of his cock and was continuing to move inside Ricky to give the young man his completion as well.

The doctor had not been overjoyed to have had to wait around for Ricky to complete his dining room supper service before collecting his fee for examining the body of the actor, Tony Taylor, in the Alexander the Great Suite hours before and writing out an accidental death certificate for a burst heart.

"He probably worked out too hard at too old an age to maintain that body of his," the doctor had said. "He died much too young, but he was a coronary waiting to happen for a few years." Overby had lovingly handled the body, wishing that he'd had access to the actor when he was alive—not that Overby had any inclination to fuck the dead. But handling the body had made him horny for having some young ass between his thighs. Ricky had been offered to him, and he'd been pleased. He just had to wait for it longer than he wanted. So, despite there being someone else waiting for Ricky's services, Overby had fucked him twice, both times from behind, the first time in a classic Doggy, and the second in the more sensual Basset Hound, where Ricky was more active in moving under the doctor and making love to the cock with the muscles of his ass channel.

Having waited longer than Dr. Overby had for Ricky's servicing and having paced back and forth impatiently in the Oscar Wilde Parlor, still on the phone making arrangements for the paperwork on the natural death of Tony Taylor in a bit of a troublesome unnatural place and position, Detective-Lieutenant David Pollack nearly pushed the doctor aside at the door of the Harvey Milk Room as the doctor was exiting and he was entering in his need to get at the luscious Hispanic waiter/room attendant cum male whore.

Ricky was still on his stomach on the bed, his feet on the floor, mellowed out by just having shot his load, when the angry and impatient policeman pounced on him. Without bothering to change Ricky's position much, Pollack dissipated his anger at the wait by grabbing Ricky by the hair and arching his torso back, with Ricky, giving a little cry of surprise, burying his hands in the bedspread at each side. Pollack entered Ricky's ass strongly in a rough Rear Entry version of the Teaspoons position, the passage

176

having been opened wide by the doctor. With his other hand, he rhythmically slapped Ricky on the buttocks.

Ricky's laughs and begging for more, deeper, faster inflamed Pollack's arousal but concomitantly evaporated his anger. The detective finished himself in another Rear Entry position, with Ricky's chest draping down off the end of the bed. Ricky supported his weight on bent and spread arms. By raising his ass a bit and using his knees on the bed for leverage, he managed to raise his pelvis to a good angle for deep penetration and a long slide. Kneeling behind him on the bed and between Ricky's spread legs, Pollack held Ricky's hips and fucked him at great length to a very satisfying ejaculation.

Both the doctor and detective left the inn satisfied that they had been well paid for their services—the doctor's medical services; the detective's protection services—and knowing that they had regular privileges at the house. Sean was turning their interests from himself to Ricky, who was becoming increasingly proficient as a male whore. He certainly was willing to add that to his job at the inn as waiter and room attendant. He was being assigned to the deputy mayor as well, and Sean had moved him out of the shared Chris Steele Room to the Harvey Milk Room that Chris Clarke had vacated so that Ricky could more easily service his growing list of clientele with regular privileges.

Although he couldn't pinpoint when it had become intentional, Sean was finding arrangements for others who once had been regulars in his bed and had now not been with anyone other than his business partner, Alex, for more than a month.

Alex' cocking was more than enough for him.

"Yes, master, yes. Pull them out and slam your dick in there. Please. Fuck me, please."

"All in good time, Chris," Eddie whispered in the young man's ear. "We have all night." He had pulled the handle of the string of graduated beads and brought the last, biggest, one to the surface. Chris groaned as Eddie coaxed the bead back inside.

"Give me your cock. I want you so bad," the rentboy, Chris Clarke, whimpered.

"Not as dull as all those johns you've serviced gave you, is it?" Eddie whispered close to Chris' ear. He had the young man in the splits on two parallel bars. Chris was naked. His legs were bound in an Elevated Split position on the nearest, lower bar, and his arms were stretched out and bound on the farthest, slightly higher bar. His nipples were pinched in tit clamps linked by a chain, which Eddie jerked on when he wanted to hear Chris yelp, and the young man's ball sac was laced tight with a leather strap, with weights distending it down toward the floor. He was hard, dripping, and throbbing.

Eddie was dressed as before, black leather, crotchless pants, black boots, black-leather harness across bulging, strawberry-blond thatched chest. Lust-driven taut nipples. He too was hard, dripping, and throbbing.

"No, you're the best," Chris forced through set teeth, his heavy panting making the words come out in a gasp. "No one's given it to me like you have; no one has had me as high as you have. Give it to me. Please!"

Eddie laughed and slapped him on the butt, his mind going to what equipment he'd put Chris on next. As he thought of his growing obsession of breaking and using this young man, his interest in Sean Temple was receding in his brain. The guy probably would break too fast anyway, and his responses would be vanilla, not challenging and worshipful like Chris Clarke's were.

And as great as it would be to tweak his brother, Alex, did he really want to start a war in the family?

Phillip's Bar, 9:00 p.m.

Brad sat in the audience, watching the drag queens strut across the stage one-by-one, vying for a combination win in beauty and talent. Mel Duncan was glowing on stage and was the clear winner of the talent portion with his "right-on" lip-synching of a Bette Midler tune. He won for beauty in his age class too, but there was no competing with youth in this or with Filipino entrants. Still, Mel got two trophies and was sparkling in the warmth of the applause that had greeted him.

Brad hadn't thought that much one way or the other about this transvestite thing. As long as they still had dicks and holes, he'd fuck the holes. When they transitioned to vaginas, he'd give a pass. But he wouldn't distain or disparage them. He just couldn't get it up without knowing there was another dick involved. Besides, he was an ass man all the way. Even if he was asked to fuck one with a vagina—and he was so grateful for having found a permanent home with GayLords that he'd probably do it if asked—he'd have to pump himself up first and do it quick. He'd still fuck them in the ass. He was definitely an ass man.

Watching the effect on Mel of being a woman for some short time, though, made Brad fully accepting of the man. He was a good lay regardless, and, at his age, if he could find something that would send his arousal up to the rafters, more power to him.

Mel had asked Brad to come and watch the contest—and then to fuck him in one of the dressing rooms afterward as Jack Wilder had done two months

179

previously. That had been memorable for Mel, and he felt that having another man other than Jack do him this way would help Mel in emotionally giving Jack up as a sex partner. Mel had been a little hurt at how easily Jack had transitioned out of being a sex partner just into being a law partner and a friend.

Duncan had booked the dressing room and Brad had readily agreed to the plan. Mel wasn't just a client of the inn's—he would have done the same as part of the B&B servicing—but Brad also had grown fond of the older man and wanted to help him achieve the pleasures he sought. And Mel was generous with his tip money.

After Mel left the stage, Brad had another drink, while Mel talked with his admirers and basked in their attention. When he walked backstage to the dressing room Mel had booked, he found Mel outside the door, in the embrace, and being kissed by a man looking not much younger than Mel was. He looked the rugged type and in good shape and was wearing army fatigues, complete with combat boots.

"Oh, Brad," Mel said when they'd come out of the clutch and Mel saw Brad standing there. "I hope you don't mind. The major says he wants to spend some time with me in the dressing room. He says he'll do it in is combat boots. I know . . . but I hope . . ."

"No problem," Brad said. "Maybe in the morning at the inn, if you want it then." Then, turning and looking at the soldier, he said, "Treat her right. She's a great lay, but she deserves to be treated right."

As he left, he was speculating whether this officer had come over from the Aberdeen Proving Grounds in Maryland. Their male brothel had been shut down a couple of months earlier. An army major would be a good possibility for a regular client at GayLords. He'd have to tell Alex and Sean about that. Already he was feeling like an integral part of the GayLords family.

"Yes, yes, like that, move your pelvis . . . like that, sweetie."

"Oh, God, you're in so deep," Joshua murmured. "Deeper than . . Tony . . . ever got. And so thick."

"I'm not so old that I can't keep it up. It's the last thing on me that will wrinkle up, I should hope," the jeweler, Dieter Baber, answered, with a small laugh. "God gave me a good one. I know he wants me to keep it hard as long as possible—and to use it."

"Oh, God, oh, God, he sure did give you a great one. You're longer and thicker than Tony was. Who would have known—?"

"Just keep fucking yourself on it like that, Joshua. You come first, and then me."

"Can't we try to come together? That's what Tony and I tried to do. Oh, fuck, it's so much better without a rubber."

"At our ages we should care about catching something that will kill us after we're naturally dead? Skin sliding on skin is best, yes. Feel those veins? I've been told it has great-feeling veins. Just keep fuckin' my cock. We'll try to come together. Peter and I worked at coming together too."

"This is the same position Tony and I were in when—"

"Don't think about it that much just now. Remember him, of course. But he's gone and you're not. Keep thinkin' about living—and getting good fucks. You can't honor him in memory if you're gone too. Get right back on the horse was what people told me when I lost Peter. And I found that to be true. I find you to be such a sweet piece of ass too. So tight at first and then open right up for me. Age don't make any difference. Get back on that horse. You're ridin' a horse's cock now. Live in the moment. Ride, ride, ride. We'll both talk about our lost ones later—you about Tony; me about Peter—when there's no ride left in us tonight."

And ride on they did, groaning and straining, fucking in the Seesaw position, both sitting on the bed, Joshua facing Dieter and in his lap, on his cock, the two rocking against each other in a seesaw motion, with Dieter rhythmically jacking off Joshua's cock to the rhythm of rocking.

They achieved a mutual launching that time and collapsed in coos and purrings, for a moment thinking of what they each had found rather than what each had lost.

Later, as they lay in close embrace and before they fucked again, they reminisced about their lives and about all of the men each had been with—most gone now, but with Dieter helping Joshua pull memories out and being helped by Joshua, in turn, they were able to remember and talk about far more than each alone would have been capable of doing.

Two old men, who had found each other, and would no longer need to beg sex off younger, grasping men.

Rock Hudson Suite, 9:00 p.m.

Meanwhile, up on the attic floor, two young, cut, virile, vigorous, and flexible men, new to gay sex and newer too to the joys of the male Kama Sutra, were busy expanding their repertoire of enjoying each other sexually.

With a laptop tuned to the gay male Kama Sutra sexual intercourse positions guide Alex had indexed for them, they were trying out some of the more strenuous positions. The current one was the Cowboy Standing, with Tye athletically cantilevering his body up from the floor to the top of the dresser. His lower calves were pressed to the dresser top, and his body went straight back toward the floor, with his weight being supported on his arms, bent over toward the floor behind his head in reverse and his hands palm down on the floor, fingers pointed at the dresser.

Standing over Tye's stomach, his hands reaching back to grip Tye's buttocks to help keep the black stud in his precarious position, Scott's ass was skewered on Tye's cock and he was rising and falling on it, as Tye's hard cock slapped against his belly.

Getting into the more athletic positions, they'd already gotten each other off in the Launch Pad position, a form of the Missionary position with Scott on the bed, legs spread, and Tye, standing on the floor, pumping Scott in a straight-on fuck. In the Launch Pad, though, Scott's feet were pressing into Tye's pecs, and when Tye announced his big shot, Scott launched Tye backward with the thrusts of his feet. This done, Tye sank to his feet between Scott's legs, now hooked on Tye's shoulders, and submitted to Scott in a Throat Swab, deep-throat blow job.

After they'd rested a bit, Tye got to pick a position from the Web site. Scott had picked the Cowboy Standing to test Tye to the limit. Tye picked the Pyramid, Placing Scott on his back, legs thrust over his head and spread, thighs pressing into his chest, hands gripping Tye's arms, as Tye rode high on Scott's "toward the ceiling thrust" ass, Tye's arms pressed into the bed above Scott's head and his legs extended widespread out to the side.

Scott picked out the Pile Driver Reverse for the next position but while they rested from the Pyramid, they lay in each other's embrace and talked of how fortunate it was that Alex, the owner of inn had taken them in hand— literally—out at the pool today and started their instruction in achieving higher and hard pleasure and bigger explosions with each other.

"Of course he told us to feel free of using any of the staff and any willing guests while we were here." Tye said.

"Except for him, unfortunately." Scott said, with a sigh.

"Yeah, except for him and his partner, Sean Temple," Tye said. "That Sean is sexy. I wouldn't mind doing him."

"You'd do someone other than me?" Scott responded, a touch of surprise mixed with hurt in his voice.

"Be honest, you'd let that Alex fuck you if he said he wanted you. He's a hunk and a half, and didn't you see the cock on that man? He's bigger than I am. I saw the way you eyed him."

Yes, Scott would have let Alex fuck him. He was a brute. So was Tye, and that was what had attracted Scott to him. But Alex was much more of a brute. And he knew all of these melting Kama Sutra positions. Truth be known, he'd thought of Alex fucking him there at the beginning, before Alex showed up to give them instruction—when Tye was squirming around on top of him, trying to get it in. He didn't think of Alex so much now. Tye was doing him real good now.

"He told us that variety was good—especially at the beginning. That eventually it was good to settle down with one man, but that variety was good to decide who the one man was and for it to stick. That, like for you and me, doing it with others would help us tell each other what we liked doing and having done to us. Haven't you seen anyone working here—other than the forbidden Alex—you'd like to have between your thighs?"

"Either the handyman, Raif, or the masseur, Hakim," Scott answered in a tentative voice, but without hesitation. He'd obviously given it prior thought.

"At least you'd keep to black bulls," Tye said, with a laugh. "I'd like to do that small Hispanic, Ricky. He's sexy as hell and I bet would scream good with a big, black cock inside him. Now, I'm ready again, if you are. Now, go over to that armchair and go down on it on your shoulders, your back running up the back of the chair and your legs spread wide. Give me an wide-open hole and I'll mount you in reverse and give you one great Pile Driver Reverse. Let's both come this time. You can jack yourself."

The Freddy Mercury Suite, 9:00 p.m.

Raif had just completed a Pile Driver Reverse of his own, his dreadlocks flailing and his hand rhythmically slapping plump, deeply tanned buttocks on the defense contractor CEO and Brazilian, Felippe Martinez. Still very flexible at his age and overwhelmed at the burst of the dam of his succumbing to gay male sexual activity, Felippe was sucking the bulb of his own cock in an Autofellatio.

Moving out of the Pile Driver Reverse position before either of them ejaculated, Raif moved into the Brazilian sucking him off, putting Felippe on his back, straddling his chest, his legs tucked under Martinez' shoulders, and force feeding him with his cock in a Fuck Face position. At this point, Hakim came in from across the room, where he'd been watching the action and working his cock. He sat on the bed, big, black cock in hand, and leaned over and swallowed the Brazilian's big, black cock, while Raif continued to force feed Felippe's throat with his own big, black cock. Felippe clutched Raif's buttocks and moaned in ecstasy, freed of all of his cares and the limits he'd put on himself, at least for the moment.

Three big, black cocks working in tandem to give each man the maximum of ecstasy.

Raif came, creaming Felippe's throat and then rolled off the Brazilian, giving the control over to the black Egyptian, Hakim, as he went to the chair Hakim had vacated and sat and watched the continued action.

Lying on his back on the bed, his head over the foot of the bed, Hakim instructed Felippe to crouch at the end of the bed, facing away from the Egyptian, and to spread his cheeks with his hands and sit on Hakim's face, while the big Egyptian ate his ass out in an Adam's Ecstasy position. Raif came back over then, took Felippe's cock in his mouth, and covering Felippe's hands with his, gave him a Usual blow job to the Brazilian's shooting of his load.

Martinez was breathing heavily at this point, so Hakim finished himself inside Felippe with a version of the Screw, the Brazilian lying on his side on the bed, and Hakim kneeling behind him, Felippe's right leg on Hakim's right shoulder and Hakim's right hand palming Felippe's left pectoral, as Hakim fucked him deep and Felippe stroked his cock with his left hand, the two of them reaching climax at nearly the same time.

The Brazilian lay there on the bed, arms and legs askew, his legs as spread as possible to relieve the ache in his nuts. He hadn't come this much in a session since his father's chauffeur had covered him and screwed him repeatedly through the night while his parents were in Europe. And then the next night . . . and the next night . . . and the next one.

Not since then had he felt so . . . finished.

He just lay there and moaned—and remembered—and wondered why he had given that up so completely, while Raif and Hakim dressed.

At the door, Raif turned and asked, "Are you going to be OK? I hope we didn't—"

"You were both spectacular. Are you available tomorrow at 3:00 for a massage, Hakim?"

"I believe so, yes. Do you want me to——?"

"I want it all. I want you to fuck me hard. And can you both come back tomorrow night to do this again?"

"I think so," Raif answered. "I'll check the schedule that Brad keeps. But may I ask a question, mon?"

He went ahead and asked it before Martinez could respond. "Earlier today you were with Brad and Chris. Tonight you took black cock. Is there a reason you want black cock tomorrow too?"

"Yes, there's a reason," Felippe answered quietly. "It has to do with memories—and I'm still working away a bit of worry."

Raif didn't ask for a further explanation. When he and Hakim were gone, Martinez lay there, lost in his thoughts. He'd had the prejudice fucked out of him. It no longer was a worry that his son was being fucked by a black bull. It now was that Felippe was fantasizing about Tye himself. Watching Tye fuck his son at the pool earlier today and seeing Tye's body and how heavy he hung, Felippe now was dreaming of getting some of that for himself. He'd never do it, of course, while Scott and Tye were together—but maybe, some day, circumstances would change. In the meantime he would search out other black bulls to satisfy him.

The Brian Boitano Suite, 9:00 p.m.

The door was a jar to the suite and Brad could hear Adam Vance moaning and Neal Ehlers grunting, so he pushed the door open and walked in.

"You started without me," he said. His view was of Adam on his shoulder blades, with his back running up the foot of the bed, legs splayed, and Neal standing over him, butt to bed, and fucking down into Adam's ass.

187

"You'd have had to come more than an hour ago to get in on the start," Neal said. "This little piece wants to fuck like a bunny."

Brad was aware of Adam's flightiness. Probably an occupational hazard of male fashion models, he guessed. He did have a good, if very slim body, though, Brad thought, and the fashion photographer was hard bodied too along with having interesting tattoos and piercings. Brad could see now that he even had a thick ring in the bulb of his cock. Adam seemed to be enjoying that.

"So, you want me to sit off to the side until I get a turn? You wanted me to come up here."

"I think Adam wants you to work right in with us, right, Adam?"

"Yes, both of you. Inside me. Together," Adam answered in a wheezy voice.

"A double?" Brad asked. "Sure he can take it?"

"Oh, yes, Adam can take it. But here, you aren't hard," Neal said when Brad had stripped down. "Come on over here and stand on the bed while I'm fuckin' this sweet hole and I'll take care of you too."

So, Brad stood up on the bed, feet on the edge of the foot of the bed on either side of Neal's body, and placed his hands on Neal's head, at the photographer sucked his cock, gripped his buttocks, and worked fingers into Brad's ass, while continuing to fuck down into Adam. It didn't take long to harden Brad up. Neal had a bead in his tongue that did a real job on the underside of Brad's cock.

It also did a job on Brad's own tongue and on his throat and his nipples as he stood on the floor facing Neal and in Neal's embrace, as both he and Neal had their cocks working in countermotion inside Adam's channel.

Brad didn't last long in this position either, as Neal's cock ring was rubbing up and down the underside of Brad's cock as they worked the ass.

They did a second DP with Brad lying on the bed, legs extended to the floor, with Adam doing a Cowboy on him, facing him, and then Neal coming in behind Adam, working his way inside. This time his cock ring was working the top of Brad's cock.

Later, as they lay in a triple embrace, Brad asked a favor. "I've never been fucked with a PA cock ring before. Could . . . ?"

Neal fucked him in a Doggy Twisted position, with Brad's chest to the bed, his butt elevated with him up on his knees, and with Adam under his pelvis and sucking his cock. Neal stood over him at the side, fucking down into him sideways, pulling his arm up into Neal's chest, and Neal's foot pressing at the back of Brad's neck.

Brad liked the effect of the cock ring caressing his passage walls even more than when he'd sucked Neal cock to get him to agree to this position and when he'd shared Adam's passage with Neal.

The Elton John Suite, 10:00 p.m.

After a long day of alternating between fucking Kurt and resting and fucking Colin and eating and fucking them both and resting and fucking Kurt and going for a swim and then eating and fucking Colin and resting, the grocery store king, Frank Hosler, had gotten around to fucking them both again.

In the process, they had been graduated and been anointed. Kurt was now the deli section chief at his store and Colin headed up the produce section at his store. For the graduation ceremony, Frank gave the two their choice of suck and fuck position. To his groaning surprise, they chose the Snake Charmer, which had the not-all-that-flexible Frank doing an elbow stand with the help of his two young helpers. It was like a head stand, but he was on his elbows instead, head down, legs extending from his

189

hips, knees bent, and a young man kneeling on either side of him, supporting his reversed, vertical body with one hand on a buttocks and the other holding his arms steady. The nice part for Frank was that the two were working his pubes, balls, and cock with their tongues until he came for them.

They then moved into a Fuck and Suck session, with the two young men 69ing each other, one over, one under, while Frank moved from one end to the other, alternating sticking it to both of them. In a Fuck Blow Sandwich position, then, Frank fucked Kurt against the wall, with Kurt's rump jutting back to Frank, while Colin knelt under Kurt and blew him. At the end of this Frank blew his wad and hobbled over to a chair to sit and watch Kurt and Colin finish each other in a 69 Standing, with Kurt standing and Colin draped down his front in reverse, his legs thrown over Kurt's shoulders and his hands gripping Kurt's calves, as the two sucked each other's cocks and balls and ate out each other's ass until, working together, they achieved a mutual orgasm, finishing this way just to show how good the section chiefs of Frank's grocery store empire could suck and fuck.

The Foyer, 11:45 p.m.

Brad had waited around for Mel Duncan to return from Phillip's Bar. It was later than he thought Duncan would be. Should I have stayed at the bar to see her safely back to the inn, he wondered. But he couldn't very well have waited this long. He had duties at the inn in the evening and was responsible for locking up. And he didn't want her to think he was her babysitter.

And then there she was, walking through the front door. She looked a bit disheveled. Her wig was a little awry and the buttons to her dress weren't aligned correctly. Brad moved toward Mel, ready to ask her if she was OK, but then he saw the gleam in her eyes and the smile on her lips where the lipstick was smudged over onto her cheek.

"The evening . . . the army officer?" Brad asked quietly.

"Forceful." Mel answered. "He took no prisoners. The gates of the city were assaulted and breached. Women were raped and put to the sword. Bodies were pillaged."

Brad was about to say something without quite knowing what to say, but Mel continued.

"He was ravenous in his victory. I surrendered gladly and denied him nothing. He asked for my telephone number and I gave him the number to my private line. Do you think I was wrong to do so?"

"Not if he brought you pleasure."

"He had me six ways from Sunday. If there's a nasty version of Alex' Kama Sutra positions, the major has mastered them."

"Do you wish to be alone tonight, or do you want company?" Brad asked. "I could come upstairs with you and stay the night. We could just cuddle if you're exhausted."

"I would like that, Brad. Thank you."

"And, if you wish, I could wake you up with a fuck."

"I would like that too."

The Diesel Washington Room, Midnight

"Yeah, it's open. Come in."

Scott had been standing outside of Raif's bedroom door for three minutes, building up the courage to knock—wondering if Raif was there; half hoping he wasn't, because going for other cocks than Tye's was a big step for him.

191

In the room now, and closing the door behind him, Scott gulped. Raif was propped up on pillows against his headboard, smoking a cigarette with one hand and fondling his cock with the other. He was naked, his body magnificent in Scott's eyes. He had his cock at half erect, but Scott could clearly see that it was headed toward full erection now.

Scott was wearing one of the inn's fluffy robes—and nothing else.

"You naked under that robe, mon?" Raif asked.

"Yes," Scott managed, with another gulp.

Raif twisted his torso and crushed his cigarette out in an ashtray on his nightstand. His other hand continued working his cock.

"You know what you've come here for?"

"Yes, I think so."

"I'll leave you exhausted and totally fucked."

"I hope so."

"Drop the robe and come here," he growled.

Raif took his time—and his pleasure—opening up Scott and preparing him first, in a Head Rush position, with Raif sitting on the side of the bed, Scott's back on his thighs, and Scott's legs spread, being supported by his hands gripping his thighs, while Raif sucked his cock and balls and ate out his ass. This was followed by an Oral Therapy position, with Scott on his back on the bed, Raif on his knees beside the bed and pinning Scott down with an arm thrown over the young man's torso, Scott's legs bent and spread, and Raif sucking Scott's cock hard and finger fucking his ass with three fingers.

By now Scott was begging for the fuck and was completely open to Raif, who dragged Scott half off the bed at the end, with Scott's torso cantilevered toward the floor, propped up on his elbows. Reversed on him, his toes pressed in the floor on either side of Scott's torso, and his hands gripping Scott's ankles, Raif fucked down in the young man's ass at the reverse with a thick, black cock in the Bumper Cars position. Before he let Scott puddle to the floor with a totally fucked moan, Raif picked him up, draped Scott's body on his front, held him in place with a full Nelson and finished him with a Bully fuck.

As Scott, groaning, pulled himself off the floor, Raif said, "You think you'll be back for more tomorrow night?"

"Yes," Scott answered. It was a pained yes, but it also was a determined and needy yes.

The Harvey Milk Room, Midnight

Tye drew a deep breath and entered the room upon Ricky Sanchez' bidding to come in.

At the door, Tye had knocked and Ricky had asked who was there.

"It's Tye Grant . . . from the Rock Hudson room."

"Come on in."

Tye entered. As with Scott, he was wearing nothing but a fuzzy inn robe. As with Raif—except for the cigarette—Ricky was propped up on his bed, naked, and fondling his cock. He had his legs spread and a dildo half up his ass passage.

"You're the young black stud Alex was giving fuck pointers to this afternoon, aren't you?"

"Yes, I'm here with the white guy who was at the pool with me. Alex said we needed to do variety."

"And you'd like to do this variety with me?"

"Among others, yes. Are you available?"

"Open your robe and show me your cock. Very nice. Hard."

"How could it not be, coming in here and seeing you like this."

"You can come over here and fuck me if you want," Ricky said. "You've got a nice hard body."

193

The two worked each other up in a 69 Sideways, with them Yin-Yanged together in a ball, each sucking the cock and balls of the other and eating each other out. They fucked initially in a Butterfly, Ricky on his back, his legs streaming around Tye's hips, and Tye with his knees pushed under Ricky's buttocks and his cock in deep and churning, but after a few minutes and for the big explosion, Ricky got fucked in the Afternoon Delight position Tye had looked at on the laptop just before coming here and was dying to try out. Ricky was suspended in the air, back to the dresser, his arms in back of his body, gripping the dresser edge, and his legs running up Tye's chest and over his shoulders, while Tye gripped Ricky's neck with one hand and his throat with the other, and stared hard down into Ricky's eyes as he thrust again and again and again with long, deep slides, into Ricky's ass.

Afterward, in a voice of awe, Ricky said, "You are one big black cocksman, and you've learned a lot in one afternoon. Feel free to come back to me tomorrow night."

"I will," Tye answered. "I think Alex was right about variety improving performance."

The Christopher Isherwood Suite, 1:00 a.m.

It was Missionary exotica night in Sean Temple's bedroom. The two started off with blow jobs and ass munching that zeroed into a full 69. Sean Rode the North Face on a loveseat in the sitting room, with Alex and the floor, his back to the front of the loveseat, and Sean kneeling in the loveseat, facing the back and sitting on Alex' face. In turn, Alex rode the South Face, with Sean taking the position Alex had had on the floor in front of the loveseat, and Alex suspended over his upturned face, steadying himself with handholds on the loveseat's arms on either side and his feet planted on Sean's bent knees. His ass rode Sean's face.

Both of them in the mood, Alex carried Sean into Sean's bedroom, made him grip the top edge of the dresser, with his body suspended straight out into space, and Alex gripped and spread Sean's legs, supporting them on his shoulders, and, pressing his face into Sean's buttocks, resumed sucking his cock and balls, and eating out his ass and slapping his buttocks in a 69 Standing position.

Their preparations for a long and vigorous fuck session were concluded with a 69 Sitting position, with Alex slouched in a tub chair in the bedroom and Sean above him, reversed on his body. Alex squeezed Sean's butt cheeks open while he ate out and finger fucked the smaller man's ass. At the end near the floor, Sean was gripping Alex' calves and sucking his cock and balls.

Alex did Sean on the bed in various athletic Missionary variations, moving from Classic Missionary, with Sean on his back and rubbing his heels on Alex' buttocks while Alex lay between his legs and fucked him slow and deep, to the Mirror of Pleasure, with Alex standing below the foot of the bed, dick deep inside Sean's ass, Sean on his back, and Alex holding Sean's legs together and off to the side to create a tight ass passage for a closer fuck, to a Missionary Inverse, with Sean on top, his torso hovering over Alex' and his arms spread and gripping the top edge of the headboard and with Alex gripping and pulling Sean's butt cheeks apart and thrusting up inside him.

Keeping to wanting a tight fuck near the end, Alex pulled Sean's buttocks to the end of the bed. He had pulled his belt out of his trousers earlier and now used it to strap Sean's thighs together. He lifted Sean's legs straight up and held the smaller man's ankles together as he worked his thick cock into the now-constricted hole and listened to Sean's moaning, Alex then fucked Sean tight in a Deep Stick position.

At Alex' command, Sean took control of the final salvo leading up to a mutual ejaculation. In the Mastery Kneeling position, Alex laid on his back at the foot of the bed, feet on the floor and arms extended out straight from his body, while Sean sat, facing him, on the cock, leaning back, with his hands on Alex' knees and fucked himself on Alex' cock in rising and falling, revolving, and rocking forward and back positions.

They lay in a side split later, Sean's buttocks spooned into Alex' groin, Alex' hand cupping Sean's chin and controlling their occasional kisses while whenever his cock threatened to go soft inside Sean, Alex' hips provided a couple of deep thrusts to keep them both on the edge of heat and as a signal to Sean that the night of fucking wasn't over.

"You sure had a lot to give tonight," Sean murmured, pulling himself back from sleep, because there was something he wanted to tell Alex—something he was afraid of discussing with Alex.

"I saved it all for you. And I haven't used it all. I'm not finished screwing you tonight."

"You haven't screwed the help or any of the guests today? You were out there with those luscious but barely men at the swimming pool. You didn't screw Scott Martinez then or later?"

"No I did not. Scott is a real temptation. So is his father, for the matter, but I left them alone. I wanted to nail you good tonight."

"And so you have. I have a confession," Sean said. It wasn't what he really wanted to discuss with Alex, but it would be a lead in, just as Alex saying he hadn't screwed anyone else today—if Alex was leveling with him, and he had sounded sincere.

"Yeah, I think I know what it is. Chris is gone. You've managed to close down our granting outside rentboys hourly access with clients."

"Do you mind, really?"

"Not really. I can see your point. It was putting us at more risk."

"We're still at risk," Sean said. "We had to give privileges to another city official today. The deputy mayor."

"He's a bastard. And maybe we should take some photos of him and Pollack—to keep them faithful."

"I'd rather not get into that. Once someone says we've photographed them, our reputation for providing privacy will be shot. I've turned them all over to Ricky."

"He'll like that," Alex said. "Little vixen can't get enough of men's cocks."

"He certainly likes that he gets his own room now. I gave him Chris' room, the Harvey Milk."

"Good. You say you've assigned all those with privileges—Pollack, the deputy mayor, the doctor to Ricky. You aren't servicing them yourself?"

"No. You haven't noticed? I haven't lain with anyone but you for weeks." And here it was, the opening.

"Not even Eddie?" Alex' voice had hardened. Sean could hear the competitiveness in the voice. He didn't know why the two brothers were so competitive. But then again, he didn't have any brothers himself.

"No, not even Eddie. Chris has gone with him."

"Ah. Bad news for Chris maybe, but not for us. I was worried about you with Eddie."

"What do you mean?"

"I hope you never find out." It was curious, Alex thought. Sean had slept with Eddie. Alex didn't know what Eddie did in fucking Sean, but Alex knew what was in Eddie's basement and what Eddie did with it and Alex had seen some of the toys Eddie had used with Sean. Sean

197

had seen Eddie's basement, and Alex had had in the back of his mind that maybe Eddie was doing that to Sean and Sean liked it. But Sean sounded so innocent on the subject of Eddie. He was exhausted the morning after Eddie had been on him, but maybe that was just how often they fucked, how deep Eddie got his big cock up into Sean, and how exotic the toys were that Sean let Eddie use on him. Maybe Eddie's basement hadn't registered with Sean. Well, maybe Eddie was out of the picture now and Sean was safe.

And Sean had said he hadn't been fucked by anyone other than Alex himself for the last month.

"Alex. Are we going to make it?"

"The inn is doing fine," Alex answered.

The wasn't really what Sean was asking, but Alex was off and running on that.

"The staff has settled down. They all work well together. And they all seem to be grateful to be here and able to do what they like sexually. There are few other places they could work without being pimped out."

"Well, we do pimp them out," Sean commented.

"They always have a choice. We wouldn't make them do anything they wouldn't enjoy. They are all randy bastards, ready to fuck at the drop of a hat."

"Yes, I guess they are," Sean agreed. "Ricky, for instance, seems delighted by the clients we've assigned to him."

"Raif and Hakim would happily fuck anything we pointed them at. And Brad has worked out the best find of the lot. Not only is he crackerjack at reception, but he also has a way with the guests. He helps lead them to where they want and need to go even if they don't realize that they came here aching for that."

"But do we do enough good?"

"We provide a free environment for men to do what they want to do without harming anyone else. We release their ability to have pleasure and to get the most out of life," Alex answered. "Look at what we've done for the Martinezes. All that those young men—barely men— knew when they came here was that they desired to have sex with each other. They didn't know how to make the best of it. They are of age; they have a right to make that decision for themselves. We helped them learn to maximize their relationship. And Scott's father. Not only did Brad stave off the tragedy of the family breaking up over the father's worries and his own hang ups, but Felippe Martinez has been sexually freed to live the life he always desired. And we can help him do that in private, if he wishes.

"It's the same thing with Mel Duncan. Brad has freed him to be what he wants periodically—and he doesn't have to give up his other life to be there.

"And the guests are involved, as well. There are two old men up in the Cole Porter Suite now, most likely happily in each others' arms. Probably even sexually satisfying each other—not only now but into the future. Baber came here having suffered a loss. Sinclair suffered his while he was here. But they have found each other here and they will heal because they were here and we made all of this possible for them."

"Yes, I see that. But it probably will be good if we don't have a death every two months."

Alex laughed. "Yes, that would be very good. For one thing we wouldn't have to pander to Dr. Overby and Detective Pollack as much. But there's another good thing that's been happening."

"Oh, what is that?" Sean asked.

"I don't know if you want to hear it. But it gives me hope that maybe it's time to talk about it now that Eddie is gone and you've mentioned not being fucked by anyone but me for a month."

"I think I do want to hear it." Sean had an inkling where this was going. It was what he had wanted to discuss and had been afraid to bring up.

"In all of this fucking all over the inn and the musical beds of sex partners, I've found I've become a bit possessive of you," Alex said, almost in a whisper, a but haltingly. "It isn't just Eddie and a brother thing—or a dangerous brother thing. I've clutched when Overby and Pollack have gone in your room. I've felt my heart skip a beat when you smile at Raif or Hakim. I find myself frowning when you and Brad put your heads together, even when I know it's just business."

"What are you saying, Alex?"

"I'm saying I haven't fucked anyone but you for a month too. Increasingly you're the only one I want to fuck. We have a great business partnership. I'd like to work toward a more settled sexual partnership too."

"I'd like that," Sean said.

"You would? But off course we wouldn't crowd each other. If you really see anyone you want to fuck, you certainly are free to do so. And same with me. I don't want us to feel tied down."

"Oh, I agree," Sean said. He was happy that it was dark in the room and Alex couldn't see how broadly he was smiling. He didn't worry about himself—he'd be able to maintain a monogamous relationship. And he knew—and loved—Alex enough that he could tolerate Alex going off the reservation occasionally. But then Alex surprised him.

"Maybe as a pledge, I could stop wearing rubbers. We could enjoy raw sex. And if either of us wanted to be with someone else, we could just go back to the rubbers. No hard feelings, but we'd have to own up to it."

"Yes, yes, I would like that. I would like that a lot." Sean fought back the tears. Alex was serious. It wasn't until this moment that Sean understood how serious he was.

"You know, I'm really glad you want that, because . . . because . . ."

"Because you weren't wearing rubbers for any of tonight," Sean said. "I knew that. I just assumed you were so hot for it that you forgot them. I was enjoying it so much that I accepted the risk—and, yes, I noticed you haven't been fucking around of late. Other than me, of course."

"I think I was so antsy about not wearing a rubber even though I knew I would bring this up with you tonight that I didn't fully enjoy the barebacking. I think that—"

"Shush and roll over on your back. It's my turn to ride you. Howabout we start with a Cowboy Reverse Asian?"

"We can start wherever you like, but, as you know, I always like to finish with a Pearly Gates."

GayLords Inn Layout

GayLords Inn is a twenty-eight-room Victorian clapboard-clad mansion on Cape May's Decatur Street not more than four blocks from the Atlantic Ocean. By custom, all of the Victorian mansions in the historic part of town are painted in bright, attention-getting colors. GayLords is painted in baby blue, trimmed in shocking pink. The inn sits on two lots, the three-story, with raised basement and mansard roof attic, building is positioned on the left lot, facing the building from the street. A drive runs down the left side of the building to a brick-fenced parking lot at the back. The lot on the right is enclosed with a brick fence and includes a terrace surrounding a swimming pool, with a pool house, the main room open to the terrace, at the back of the lot.

The fourth floor is an attic, under a mansard roof. There is a square tower at the right front corner of the house and a deep porch across the front of the house. A one-story enclosed sun porch is at the left, separating the driveway from the three-story portion of the house.

There are nine rentable guest rooms, expandable to ten, and the owners' suite, all with baths. All of the principle rooms in the inn are named after famous homosexual men.

Rooms on the First, Main Floor:

Entry in the middle of the house off the front porch is into a large foyer, facing an open staircase going to the second floor. A cross hall runs beyond the foyer, behind the staircase. The cross hall extends to the outer wall on the right and provides access to the swimming pool area. The foyer goes up three stories. to the right of the foyer, at the front, including the tower space, is the Oscar Wilde Parlor. Behind that, on the right side, is the Leonard Bernstein Music Room. Behind that and the cross hall, in the back right corner, is the Truman Capote Library.

To the left of the foyer, is the Gore Vidal Dining Room, with the Michelangelo Sunroom beyond that, running the full length of the dining room and functioning as an auxiliary dining room. The kitchen is at the back, left corner of the building. The Tim Cook Office is located at the left between the dining room and the kitchen and opens onto the cross hall. There are men's and women's bathrooms off the cross hall.

The Greg Louganis Pool House is at the back of the lot on the right.

Rooms on the Second Floor:

The Freddy Mercury Suite is on the front, right corner and includes a tower room. The Elton John Suite is on the front, left corner. The Harvey Milk Room is on the left behind the Freddy Mercury Suite. The owners' triple suite, The Christopher Isherwood Suite, is across the back and extends around the right to behind the Freddy Mercury Suite.

Rooms on the Third Floor:

The Cole Porter Suite is on the front, right corner and includes a tower room. The Brian Boitano Suite is on the front, left corner. The Don Lemon Room is on the left behind the Brian Boitano Suite. The Alexander the Great Suite is across the back and extends around the right to behind the Cole Porter Suite.

Rooms on the Attic Floor:

The Chris Steele Room (beds for two of the inn's staff members) is on the front, right corner and includes a tower room. The Rock Hudson Suite is on the right behind the Christ Steele Room and has a connecting door to the Renée Richards Suite along the back of the building. The Diesel Washington Room (for one of the inn's staff members) is on the left, front, with a storage room behind it.

Rooms in the Basement:

The Tennessee Williams Wine Cellar is under the kitchen. The Jack Kerouac Billiards Room is under the dining room. The Anderson Cooper Media Room is under the parlor.

List of the 82 Gay Male Kama Sutra Positions Depicted

(Note: The named gay male Kama Sutra positions in this book are keyed to those in the Web site http://gaysexpositionsguide.com/)

369
69 Sideways
69 Sitting
69 Standing
Adam's Ecstasy
Afternoon Delight
Anal Train
Autofellatio
Basset Hound
Bent Over
Bent Spoons
Bodyguard
Bodyguard Elevated
Bulldog
Bully
Bumper Cars
Butterfly
Cowboy
Cowboy Asian

Cowboy Reverse
Cowboy Reverse Asian
Cowboy Sideways
Cowboy Splits
Cowboy Standing
Crab
Danseur
Deep Impact
Deep Stick
Doggy
Doggy Elevated
Doggy Standing
Doggy Twisted
Double Dildo
Double Header
Double Penetration
Elevated Splits
Fire Hydrant
Flying Spider
Folded Deck Chair
Fuck and Suck
Fuck Blow Sandwich
Fuck Face
Fusion
Head Rush
Jockey
Jockey Asian
Lap Dance
Launch Pad
Leg Glider
Mastery
Mastery Kneeling
Mirror of Pleasure
Missionary
Missionary Inverse
Oral Therapy

Pearly Gates
Perfecta
Pile Driver
Pile Driver Reverse
Pile Driver Sideways
Pirate's Bounty
Plumber
Pyramid
Rear Entry
Riding the North Face
Riding the South Face
Scissors
Screw
Seesaw
Sitting Bull
Snake Charmer
Soaring Eagle
Soaring Eagle Reverse
Spit Roast
Spoons
Suspended Congress
Teaspoons
The Usual
Throb Swab
T-square
Warrior
Warrior Reverse

About the Author

Habu is one of the pen names of a former supersonic spy jet pilot, intelligence agent, male model, movie actor, and diplomat. A wild youth in Southeast Asia was spent enjoying whatever sexual opportunities came his way, and much of his gay male writing is about recalling incidents from those days and inventing ones he'd perhaps have liked to experience. He now leads a very quiet and ordinary happily married family life.

An American, he is a published mainstream novelist and short story writer under another name and in another dimension of his life. He has written or cowritten (with Sabb) approaching 1,000 published short stories and over 100 published erotica e-books, primarily of gay fiction but also memoir, straight fiction and ménage fiction. His hand and creative writing can be seen in stories and books by habu, sr71plt, Dirk Hessian, Shabbu, and Stephen Kessel—among unrevealed others that might surprise readers. The fictionalized GM memoir *Flying High, Diving Deep* is loosely based on his life experiences. He can be found at the adults only gay male site www.BarbarianSpy.com, which he shares with Sabb and Dirk Hessian.

Our authors always like to receive feedback, and appreciate it when readers post reviews at distributors and other sites.

FOR LITERARY HEAT

Not all books listed below may currently be on release.
* indicates the book is available in paperback and e-book.
BOOKS BY CHRIS CROSS
Multisexual Adult Romance
Pulaski Square
Chocolate in Vanilla (MF)
Christmas with Chris (MMF) (MM) (MF)
BOOKS BY ALEX LOCKHEED
Transgender Romance
Meeting Jenna
Transgender Other
Being Sarah
BOOKS BY DIRK HESSIAN
Xtreme Historical Erotica
The King's Men
Shores of Tripoli
Prophecy of Noto
Pretender's Fate
General Historical Erotic Romance
Confederate Gold
Puttin on the Ritz
To the Hessian Hills
Fire Down the Valley*
Constantinople*
The Beautiful Way*
Blue and Gray
Colonel's Treasure

Beginning of Time
Labyrinth
BOOKS BY HABU
Gay Erotica
Memoir Faction
Flying High, Diving Deep*
Xtreme Erotica
Liaisons
Chain Gang Banged (Short Story)
Tramp Steaming*
Escape to Girne
Silas' Choice*
Last Call
Choke Hold
Apyko: The Greek Pimp
Visits of the Schlange
Second Coming: Emile La Cour Unleashed*
Vortex: Sacrificed by Curiosity*
Dark Angel Sounding *(in e-book & included in
Sounding:Ultimate Control paperback)**
Sounding: Ultimate Control (*Print Only*)*
Sounding Five *(in e-book & included in
Sounding:Ultimate Control paperback)**
Romance
GayLords Inn
Finding a New Sam
Bangkok Summer Seduction
The Photograph
Inevitable Case
Turn to Love
Rain Check
Built for Pleasure (Sci Fi)
Danny's Choice*
Pull of the Groove
Sugar n Spice Christmas
Friday Nights with Lenny (Christmas Romance)
Snowy, Snowy Nights (Christmas Romance)
Tank n Bull

Sail to the Sun
War Letters
Ravens Roost
Caribbean Cruise Top to Bottom
Arena Stage
Trading Partners (Valentine's Day)
Four Coins
Lower Than the Heart (Valentine's Day)
Brambleton
Gotta Keep Trying
Finding Amnad
Platres Conclave
Other Novels/Novellas
Fist of Gold
Syrian Ram
Temptation's Clutches*
Descent into Chaos
Escape to Girne
Journey Through Abilene
Harmony and Dissonance
Stallion Station
Racing With the Devil (espionage suspense)
Prepared in Cape Verdi
Gilded Cage
House on Park*
Anything for Ambition
Dance of the Ravishers
Hard Knocks U*
My Neighbor's Spa*
Man's Man: Tales of a High Priced Gay Hooker*
Trip Money
The Indian Doctor
Sailorboy
Home to Fire Island
Murder Mysteries
All Fools Day Foolery (Mike Kavanagh)
Inevitable Case (Mike Kavanagh)
Vanishing Laura

Death on a Ping Pong Table
Clint Folsom Mysteries Compendium Volume 1*
Death to Blonds - Stolen Judgment (Clint Folsom
Mystery)*
Clint Folsom Mysteries Compendium Volume 2*
Gay Erotica Anthologies
Earth Cry*
Shunga
Habu's Christmas Balls
Eight in D*
DevilMENt
Silas' Choices*
Stallion Station (A Novella in Parts)
Eleven to the Dogs*
Fifty Seventy*
Spy Tails 001*
Spy Tails 002*
Doubled*
Doubled Again*
Tails in the Tropics*
Tails in the Med*
Tails in the West*
Rough Riders*
Grab Bag 1*
Grab Bag 2*
Grab Bag 3*
Grab Bag 4*
Grab Bag 5*
Grab Bag 6*
Grab Bag 7*
Grab Bag 8*
Grab Bag 9*
Beyond the Beaded Curtain*
Habu's Christmas Balls
The Sporting Life*
Fetish Galore!*
Literary Gay Erotica
Cairo Surrender*

The Handyman*
Homeward Bound
Journey to Mirage*
Bisexual/Menage/Multisexual Erotica
And Eat it Too
Two Men, One Woman*
Every Which Way
Summer of Denial
Death on a Ping Pong Table
Cruising Gigolo
13 Ways for Halloween
Luther*
The Indian Prince*
BOOKS BY SABB
Driver Reliever
Hiring in Hollywood
The Legend of Holleystone Grange
Surprise Encounters*
She is He
Wrong Man
Loyal to his King
Barbarian Tales - Book One - Traveler's Tales*
Barbarian Tales - Book Two - Journeys Begin*
Barbarian Tales - Book Three - The Inheritance*
Barbarian Tales - Book Four - Road to Persepolis*
BOOKS BY SHABBU
Velvet Interrogation
Finding Jason
Dirty Pool
Operation Black Jade
Cigars!*
Angel in the Barn
Gayly Complicated*
Despoiling David
The Tree of Idleness*
I Met a Man
Rough Road to Happiness
BOOKS BY STEPHEN KESSEL

Gay Romance
The Forever Man
Two Chances
BOOKS BY KIM BLACK
Lesbian Romance
Transfixed on Tammie (F/T lesbian)